HESPARIA'S TEARS

IMOGENE NIX

ISBN 978-0-9954182-8-8

Dedication

Where do I even start? It feels like a million years since this book first released some five years ago. I've been on a roller coaster journey since then and having these rights back means so much to me.

With the passage of time, comes lots of other milestones, from learning to write with children home through to becoming "empty nesters" and having space and time to myself. As each book has emerged from its cocoon it's allowed me to play with ideas, to refine my craft and become more than I was before.

Yet, throughout all the years some things haven't changed. I still write Science Fiction, I have the best band of friends around me (both authors and non-authors) and the support of family and of course my readers. So this book is dedicated to everyone who has supported me along the way and trust me there's been heaps of them.

From Tara (Fantasia Frog) for the awesome cover design, Sassie for re-editing it. My "In The Chair" tribe of Suzi, Keri and Sassie. My bestie Tracey...

My family Mark, Charlotte, Beth (yes and Patrick too) my amazing M-I-L June and especially to the memory of my F-I-L Kevin.

I hope you enjoy this tale, set mainly in Australia... with a small snippet in New York, that features a strong female who's been damaged and finds that love opens a bigger, bolder and altogether better world for her.

Because when all is said and done, that's what romance is about.

Making the world we live in a better place.

I hope this book makes you smile too.

Imogene Nix
2019

Prologue

Jessa heard the hubbub in the courtyard as she stepped out of the bathroom. "Oh my God!" A woman's voice, high pitched and shocked, grated and Jessa noted the stunned looks on the men and women in the café.

What's going on? Jessa glanced around, catching sight of the large screen pointed toward the patrons. "Alien contact made. More details to come." The sound was turned off, but they didn't need it. The words scrolling across the bottom of the screen said it all. For a moment, a sense of unreality swept through her.

It wasn't April first, was it? As quick as the thought came it swept away and urgency filled her. I need to get back to work.

Jessa strode inside the café and ordered a coffee to go, after all, they'd likely be run off their feet, she was sure. The woman looked at her as if immobilized and Jessa had to restrain her frustration, an urge to roll her eyes rising.

"So, aliens are really coming, I never thought it would happen in my lifetime." She peered at the woman over the counter. "Are you okay?"

"They're coming... They're real."

"Well, if what the news is telling us, I guess it's real." She leaned away from the counter. "So, can I order my coffee now?"

The woman nodded and distractedly prepared the cappuccino, but still cast scared looks at the television from time to time.

Once the coffee was paid for, Jessa scooped it up and strode quickly to her small car, parked under a shady tree. It started on the first turn of the key, the motor revving quietly and she turned on the radio then indicated and pulled out.

"There's no cause for alarm." The soothing and calming voice of the woman shared. "After all, they're expected to make landfall in the United States, though there's been no response to hails."

"But how do we know they aren't interested in forcibly taking us prisoner?" Another voice—that of the commentator—asked. It's probably the question on everyone's mind.

"Realistically, we don't. My thoughts are that, if they're so technologically advanced as to be able to undertake space travel, surely they are more higher-minded. I doubt our abilities would even rate on their scale of interest." The self-satisfied tones angered Jessa.

"Like you'd even know." She muttered, changing gears smoothly as she headed for the observatory.

The commentator recapped the very few known facts, thanked the guest and reminded everyone listening to 'stay tuned and we'll share information as it comes to hand.' Jessa ground her teeth. Surely this was a joke? Her mind still wanted to find a way to dismiss it.

She drove quickly and once parked, chanced a look around, searching for Seth, her friend of many years. But he wasn't to be seen. Then again, that wasn't a surprise, he mainly worked the night shift, monitoring the equipment, while Jessa maintained the small on-site shop.

JESSA TRUDGED HOME. The airwaves were constantly filled with the updates on the security situation though very few seemed to know what the truth was. In the week since the announcement of the aliens' imminent arrival it seemed like those here on Earth still had no idea why they were coming.

Canberra was in lockdown, as were all major cities in Australia. The United States had closed its borders to all traffic, as had most countries in Europe. Every radio and television station ran wall-to-wall coverage and the people of earth waited to see what would happen.

The locals initially acted in their usual laid-back manner, until the threat loomed large, then representatives of the local church door knocked, giving people an opportunity to repent their sins. The stores were almost empty of long-life stock and she even knew of some who headed "out west" claiming they knew of deserted caves where no one would find them.

For Jessa, it was the opportunity of a lifetime. Something she had never expected to see. On the downside, strict curfews had been enacted and only those with passes were able to drive after sundown. Jessa kept hers stashed away; having had to battle to obtain one, only allowed as she worked at the observatory, but she was under strict conditions. It chafed, but at least she could come and go as necessary.

The ongoing questions swirled through the airwaves. What would they be like? Why were they coming? Most of all, would they be friendly to the humans? Of course, the television and radio broadcast twenty-four-seven with movies showing alien-human interactions and the whole Area 51 thing taking on greater importance than ever before. Documentaries were interrupted with special broadcasts calling for peace among the masses and astronomers and computer geeks were regularly interviewed to get their perspective.

Jessa parked her car in its usual spot outside the house. The lights shone and the sound emanating from within told her that her parents were watching the news. That seemed to be all they did these days. With a sigh she climbed out, locked the car behind her with a beep and headed to the door.

Thoughts of the B-Grade horror flicks from the fifties and sixties filled her mind. Are they coming here for some nefarious reason? Will they use us for slave labor or take the natural resources of the earth? She laughed at the fanciful notions even as the rumble of an army truck trundling past caught her attention momentarily. Jessa shivered. Thoughts of any form of alien war on the planet ricocheted for a moment then subsided. Surely not? But even as the thought settled, she knew, if these were their reasons for coming to earth, there was probably little humanity could do. Humans would be technologically outgunned. She shrugged.

"Jessa? Is that you?" Her mother called out as she entered the house.

Great. Frustration filled her. "Yes Mum! It's me. Not some alien intruder." The minute the words escaped, she knew they were the wrong ones to utter.

"Jessa, you shouldn't make light of this! Who knows why they've come? It could be to rape or pillage, you silly girl. Get inside before you get us all in more trouble. Then help me make dinner. Be useful for once in your life."

The blare of the television came from the lounge. She ducked in, to see her father sitting in his usual chair in front of it. "Hey Dad. Anything new?" He accepted the light kiss on the forehead with a frown then shook his head.

"No. But you'd better go help your mother." Jessa dropped her bag on the post of the steps and headed to the kitchen.

Chapter 1

The spaceship entered orbit and Jessa watched the trajectory on the television. Since learning of the existence of extra-terrestrials, it was about all most people wanted to do. See where they were and where they planned to land.

The reporter came back on the screen. "We believe they will make their landing somewhere on the continent of Australia. However, there have been no further radio communications from the craft, making Australia an educated guess right now."

Jessa giggled at the sober face of the young, twenty-something reporter standing outside the Parkes Observatory and the inane follow up comment made by the thirtyish female news anchor.

"Jessa, it's time for bed!" her mother yelled.

She sighed dramatically. At twenty-four she was no longer a child, even though her parents seemed to struggle with that small fact.

Maybe it's time to move out. As quickly as the thought crossed her mind, she dismissed it. Leaving home meant more expense than she could possibly afford. The thing that really irked? Paying an outstanding legal bill for something she hadn't even done. It was a refrain that had played through her mind over and over again since the event took place. It may have happened years ago, but she continued to pay for her youthful dalliance that she regretted.

Jessa stood before heading down the old hallway to the bathroom. Living at home meant sharing a bathroom with her little brother, Ben. Of course, being a boy of sixteen, he was disgusting. There were used razor blades, splashes of water and foam from his recent shaving experience and hairs in the sink. Knowing it would make no difference complaining about it, she carefully picked up the discarded mess and placed it all in the bin beside the vanity. Wiping away the mess was part of her nightly ritual.

Emerging from the bathroom, she spied her mother, standing at the end of the hall in her fluffy blue dressing-gown with matching slippers, and her blonde hair sitting high on her head in soft curlers. The same scene every evening. "Night Jessa."

"Night, Mum." *What else was there to say?* In a funk, Jessa entered her room, closed the door and sat on the side of the single bed. She breathed deeply, letting the oxygen flow into her lungs before levering herself down across the mattress. Her blinds were open, giving her an excellent view of the star-studded sky. It was a major positive to living on the edge of town, the absence of street and building lights obscuring the starlight.

"Whoever you are, I certainly hope you're friendly." Jessa muttered, before closing her eyes, rolling onto her side and willing herself to sleep.

Her mind couldn't settle. *Finally, visitors from the stars.* No longer was this a figment of someone's imagination or something from a science fiction novel. The time had come for them to have contact with another species. Sobering though, was the knowledge the Prime Minister had sent a radio message to the ship. *God, I hope she didn't act like her normal pompous dick self.* Jessa snuggled down and waited for the touch of sleep, her mind wandered before she drowsed.

THE CELL PHONE sitting on the bedside table buzzed and shuddered. Jessa muttered in the dark, groping for the device. She reached out and found the red leather cover and dragged it to her ears.

"'lo?"

"Jessa, it's me. Seth. Can you come to the office? I need you." His voice was full of excitement.

She squinted. "I was asleep, Seth. Besides which, I'm off duty until Saturday." The room was gloomy, and she screwed her face up into a scowl, knowing sleep would probably elude her now. "What could be so important that I need to come in in the middle of the night?" Jessa pushed back the covers, swung her legs over the side then slipped her feet into the old gray slippers beside the bed.

"I can't tell you over the phone."

"What?" *Something's happening.* The thrill of excitement grew deep in her chest and for an instant her brain warred caution even as interest spiked.

"*Jessa…*"

He didn't need to plead. She was already getting up to hunt out clothes. "Sure. Yeah, I'll be there in a few minutes."

"Thanks. You really won't regret it." The excitement in his voice was contagious.

Jessa hurriedly tapped the end call button.

THE LAND, so alien with hues of blue and green grew larger as the craft descended. "Captain, do you really intend to land here? After those transmissions?"

Galan sat in his chair, watching the view-screen, hearing the concern and horror in the voice of his second-in-command. "I do, Joras. We must remember our primary objective." The words may have sounded unconcerned, yet he too had reservations after the tone of the communications he had received from the…*what did they call themselves? Oh right, yes,* Earthlings… It was obvious they had no imagination, calling themselves that. Especially the woman who had called herself the Prime Minister, whatever that was. But piquing his interest was the other transmission he'd received—the young man, who had called himself Seth. He sounded like he might be a possible go-between for them, something his people had always found helpful in the past when dealing with new planets and species.

Frustration pulled at him as he rose from his seat, making his way to the navigator's position. "How long until landing?"

"Sir, on our current course, I estimate no more than three *horanas*." Galan nodded. Three *horanas* to prepare. It wasn't much, but it would have to do. "Joras, have your security team ready and fully briefed. We'll have to treat this as an ambassadorial meeting. I will prepare a communiqué for our Liege, concerning our position and plans." He turned back to his friend, rubbing a hand absently along his jaw. "Joras, when we land, I need you to remain here."

Joras opened his mouth but Galan stopped him with a look. "No. As captain, it is my right to be the one to make contact."

Joras looked at him hard, no doubt wondering at the wisdom of his decision, then nodded wordlessly. Galan turned to the automatic doors, and headed to his small office.

He felt the heavy burden of duty to his people. The state of the few remaining females on his planet weighed on him, like a heavy chain around his neck. All but fifty had passed through the gates of forever due to a problem of their scientists making. It had only just come to light in the last several *jahr*, as the women died in childbirth. Indeed all but a few children were born having already died in the womb.

The genes that had been cloned into their females had degraded, meaning they could neither reproduce, nor enjoy a full lifespan. He himself felt the burden of grief as his own partner, Gospah, had died in child birth, some fifteen *jahr* ago. She'd been among the first and the healers hadn't known the cause. Not then, anyway. It had only come to light as the waves of loss gripped his planet. He knew that Joras too faced a bleak future, with his partner Doreanh passing only three *jahr* ago. One of the reasons this ship was so ably crewed: Not one member aboard was unaffected.

The few unpartnered men of his planet needed companions and his people would die without women to share their lives.

He and his crew came seeking potential partners for the males of his kind. At least seventy, his father, the ruler had requested, but he knew better than that. Seventy would only make the situation worse, as other men would not form a partnerships and cause an imbalance. Such angst and anger on a planet known as calm and restful would be devastating.

His small home was a rock of misery with thousands of males now unpartnered. It was imperative that they convince as many females as they could find, to both replenish the gene pool and to accept a place in his world. He however, refused to allow that any force or coercion would be acceptable and every male aboard his ship had been carefully considered. This would be simply the first of many such missions, he knew.

"If I can gain agreement from the ruling government to request three hundred that would be a beginning," Galan muttered. His stomach churned. He was no fool, aware the women may not agree or the government would block their request for assistance. All those things kept him awake at night and worried him ceaselessly. True, some men had left their agrarian lifestyle to seek a life and partner on other planets. For those who remained, the future was, indeed bleak—unless they were successful in this aspect of their mission.

Of course, that wasn't the only point of the mission, though it was the most urgent. They also needed diplomatic alliances with other planets, an agrarian and pacific planet was always in far more danger when it didn't have strong alliances, his father had taught him. This was their opportunity to form one easily, or so they all hoped.

The small holographic image of Gospah, his long-departed wife, greeted him on arrival in his office. His heart ached yet he realized the pain had weathered to a dulled emotion, replacing the crushing misery he'd experienced when he'd first lost her to the forever realms.

"Gospah, I hope to bring happiness to the men of our planet. But in all I do, it is in memory of your loss." He said the words as he had every day of the long journey, making a deep obeisance as was required by their belief system. Today he wondered if it wasn't time to let her go, after all these *jahrs*.

With that thought still churning in the back of his mind, he headed to his desk and replayed the transmission from the Prime Minister of one of the continents of the Earth. *"Of course, you will need to present yourself to our facilities for negotiations…and testing."* Her tone had been condescending and irritating. But he needed their help, so he'd accept that. *For now.*

He snorted, raising his cup of serra. They had obviously never left their home, except to check out their small moon, but this section of the galaxy was a backwater anyway. He knew no other species had attempted any form of contact, otherwise, they'd have been aware that they had no right to make such demands. He'd already checked their technology to see that they hadn't evolved very far, then shook his head. "We need these people as allies so do not focus on their shortcomings, Galan."

He snorted. This would be just the first of many visits from such beings as them, once their decision was made. With that knowledge, he prepared a memory cube of information he would hand to them, containing specifications for ships and energy systems. He added a copy of the agreement all known planets had agreed to, showing the courtesies and acceptable requests governments could make of each other, with a smile.

"SETH BETTER HAVE the coffee pot on," Jessa grumbled as she slowed the car to a halt. She hopped out, into the cool late-night air and crunched across the gravel before entering the facility. "Seth?" She yelled, wincing as her voice reverberated in the emptiness.

"Yeah, I'm here." A head emerged from the room beyond. He waved his hand. "Come here…be quick."

Against her will, Jessa quickly stepped towards him, searching for signs of the coffee pot and on spying it grabbed a mug. She poured a drink before adding milk from the small fridge. "Okay. I'm here now. What?"

"They're going to land here." Seth jittered around, grabbing her attention with his wild movements and gyrations.

She stared at him. *Who? Who was going to land here?*

"I made contact on unsecured channels. Look!" He waved his hands.

She watched slack jawed as the transmission auto-extracted before her eyes. The information streamed across the screen and she made some quick calculations in her head. They were going to land here. In Parkes! Near the telescope. "Holy Mother of God. What have you done?" She whispered, awed, even as the reality of the situation hit home.

The enforcement bodies would know and would arrive any time now. This was worse than last time, when Jace had taken advantage of her. Just like last time she would be blamed. It wouldn't matter that she had nothing to do with it. The fact Seth had called her and she was currently looking at information he shouldn't have, implicated her.

She winced, remembering the believable information Jace had fabricated. She'd been stupid enough to allow him access to a secured location. Jessa gulped, fearing that it would be infinitely worse this time, if the authorities had the wrong idea about her and whatever actions Seth had taken.

"Oh man... what if the police arrest us? ASIO? Geez, I bet even the CIA and Mossad have someone on the way here right now. That's before you even consider MI5! You're mad and I'm in deep shit!" She backed away even as the sound of sirens filled the air from outside. Her stomach roiled in anticipation of the scenes ahead. "I can't afford to get in trouble again, Seth. You of all people, know that!" The accusing words flowed from her mouth before she could stop them, and he looked at her, hurt. She sighed heavily.

"I thought you'd want to be involved in this? It's not every day we make first contact."

She closed her eyes. It was too late to extricate herself now. All she could hope was that Seth was more honorable than Jace. And told the truth convincingly enough. Head aching with the reality of his ill-conceived actions, she bowed her head and listened to the sounds of movement from outside. The door burst open with a thud and her eyes reopened. The police entered, guns held in front of them. "Freeze!"

The policeman from her youth, Detective Inspector Chalmers looked at her and she shrugged uselessly. What else was there to say? *She was here, someone had made contact and she had a history.*

THE QUESTIONING WENT on and on.

"Honestly, I was in bed and didn't know anything until I got here. Seth called me. You can see that on my phone. I wasn't involved." She leaned in focusing on the hard-faced man sitting opposite her. With an aching head and people coming and going constantly, she was close to breaking point. Officers stalked around talking on cell phones, some making angry requests for information and equipment from whoever they spoke to.

They remained in the small office listening to her explanation with interest. Chalmers' voice grew more strident as it became clear that the ship would soon arrive. Even with the threat of recriminations, she admitted—privately—to a small degree of excitement. Being there when first contact was made? It would be something she'd remember forever. She shivered at the thought.

The ground started moving, shuddering beneath her feet as the walls rattled. Things on the table bounced, and a roaring sound enveloped them, growing ever louder. A policewomen hurried to the television perched on the wall and turned on the news channel. *"Look, sir! They're here."*

Jessa watched, amazed as the large ship descended. It was long and dark, perhaps best described as cigar-like with several small thrusters slowing their descent. She couldn't see any windows or viewing ports, but perhaps they were at the top? The police had been unable to keep the media away, and the live broadcast was sure to be a winner in the ratings, Jessa mused. The deafening roar of engines ceased, the ship holding steady above the ground as large stubby legs deployed slowly below, with a loud metallic screech. She absorbed each piece of information like a sponge, her eyes widening as the ship touched down on Earth and the thrusters stopped.

Silence.

The blue line of police edged closer to the reporter as everyone waited. Jessa held her breath along with everyone else in the room. At the bottom of the ship, a light shone then a platform emerged, showing fifteen people—humanoids. They could have been from Earth, except their skin was colored like a weirdly shining rainbow.

"They're coming out!" The woman reporter called, breaking the silence.

"Holy Mother of God." One of the police behind her called out. She turned, observing the rotund man crossing himself.

"We are here to meet with the one called Seth." The voice boomed through the air. A strangled sound which wasn't quite a gasp emerged from Seth, sitting on her left.

"Isn't going to happen, sunshine." The Det. Inspector intoned.

She nearly laughed at the bemused expression on Seth's face, while the woman on the television continued her inane babble.

"Our contact with Seth was acceptable and we will only deal with him and the one he calls Jessa as liaisons. We refuse to deal with anyone else." The voice boomed and people cowered.

The phone rang, just as it had incessantly since the police arrived.

A policewoman picked it up. "Sir? It's um... It's the *Prime Minister*, sir."

Jessa kept her gaze on the scene unfolding in front of her. The aliens stepped forward, the tall one who had spoken stood in the middle, and the others appeared to flank him. They looked around then with a few quick, inaudible words they headed for the building. The view on the television panned, shadowing their movements.

"They're heading to the facility itself." This time the female reporter's voice was little more than an excited squeak.

Jessa's fingers automatically moved as if to tidy her hair, the tug of the cuffs stopped her and she swore in her mind. The Det. Inspector had moved away, his voice low as he kept flicking looks to the screen.

"Do you think they're looking for us?" Seth's voice broke her concentration.

She shrugged. "I would say that's a fair bet Seth. Depends on what you've promised." Her gaze was now firmly on him.

He shrugged sheepishly. "I just told them that we're astronomers seeking an extra-terrestrial experience." His voice trailed away.

Detective Inspector Chalmers thrust the receiver back at the female and turned. "Let them in." He turned back, glowering. "I've been told you two are supposed to talk them into meeting with the government officials. Nothing more. Then once the military have arrived, you will cease to have anything to do with this."

The slow burn of anger coursed through Jessa's veins. Now that she had come this far, she refused to be shut out.

Chapter 2

He strode forward, watching as the people in blue scurried out of his way. Funny, he was a peaceful Hesparian, yet these people acted as if they feared him. He filed that away for future reference, in case it meant they were a warring race. A glassed entry stood in front of him and he watched as Joras' people moved around him, pushing at the barrier which didn't open. They conferred momentarily before putting their hand to what look like a handle and stepping back as it opened in silence. They moved around the door, waiting for him to venture within. The small building was squat with an old-fashioned bowl thing on the roof. Truly amazing how technologically backward they seemed to be.

More people milled around, looking at him with their mouths open and fearful eyes. This could become a serious problem, he conceded.

"I am Galan, and these here are my men. Where will I find the ones called Jessa and Seth?" He watched as another barrier, this to the side, opened for him. With a nod, several of his people entered quickly and he waited for the confirmation of safety. In barely a *tackard*, they came back to the door, motioning him nearer. Several steps brought him to the threshold where a big man stood watching him with an angry look on his face.

"I'm Seth." He heard the voice and glanced over the shoulder of the man in the doorway. He saw two people, a young man and woman, sitting in what looked to be a most uncomfortable manner, with their arms stretched out behind them. The woman's dainty features captured his attention. Her hair as red as the *Farbian Pearls* that were cultivated on his uncle's farm, and her skin fine and pale under the harsh lighting.

"You are Seth, and this is Jessa?" Galan indicated them and the one called Seth bobbed his head madly. Jessa, the woman, sat still, following him. He moved closer.

The big man stepped into his path. "They are prisoners. You will only talk to them from here."

He listened to the words feeling confusion. *Prisoners?* "Forgive me. They have broken a law or regulation?" If they were dangerous prisoners, then he would cease negotiating with them—that was an unwritten rule of diplomatic negotiations. The guidelines of acceptable missions were clearly delineated, but a feeling or knowledge deep within him, told him there was an inconsistency in the situation.

"They were not supposed to contact you. Especially *her.*" The angry man pointed to the beautiful woman, who sat straight and still in the chair. Strain lines appeared at the side of her perfectly formed mouth. For the first time in many *jahr*, emotions within him swirled to life when he glanced upon her face. A situation he wasn't altogether comfortable with.

"Why her?" His interest was roused.

"Because she's been involved in… trickery and illegal behavior before."

Galan settled his gaze once more on the woman, a turbulent look filled her eyes as he stepped closer. She said nothing, just raised her chin higher, as if daring him to dismiss her. He smiled at the action. She had sass going for her but there was a hint of vulnerability in her eyes. He decided to take a chance.

"We are here to negotiate. She… They will do nothing wrong. You may go now."

His dismissal obviously was not warmly received as the guard grimaced and extended a hand, attempting to stop him, no doubt. Galan sidestepped it easily as his security team shifted behind him. He stilled them with a quick motion.

"Now, see here…"

Galan turned, slowly, gaze narrowed as he bared his teeth, growling deep in his throat. The large man swallowed and stepped back. Galan didn't move.

Galan thought the guard must have decided the menacing action would be followed through as he backed away. Releasing a breath, Galan was thankful to finally be alone with his people and the two he planned to negotiate with. He advanced, noting that neither of them rose.

"You do not fear me?" Irritation flashed through him as the woman watched him in silence.

The man called Seth shook his head. "We can't exactly get up and run away. We're cuffed here." He jingled something at his back.

Galan knew a minute of icy rage, before stepping nearer to the chairs and extracting a small device from his pocket. He scanned the metal bracelets, calling forth one of the specialists who looked over his shoulder.

"Crude and unusual, Captain." The officer pulled a small sonic device from the kit he carried and dealt with the restraints. Seth sighed with relief, rubbing his wrists, but the woman only moaned, pulling slightly away from him but Galan dragged close one of the wooden chairs and sat down, opposite Jessa who watched him warily.

TRUSSED up like a prisoner wasn't her idea of how she planned to meet her first extra-terrestrial. And this one was hot. He was smoking really, if she could discount the dazzling array of colors that danced over his skin in a disconcerting manner.

"Are you… Umm… Is that your natural coloring?" *Good old Seth. You can always count on him to come out with the questions you really shouldn't ask.*

"What?" The man—they called him Galan- appeared startled for a moment then let out a chuckle. "No. It's part of the camouflage we use when travelling to a planet for the first time." The man dipped a hand into a pocket and his skin stopped glowing. His people did the same and finally, she could see them in their true color, a deep berry brown. "We find most cultures and planets think it off putting, not knowing what we are. Is that your normal color?" He lifted a hand towards them.

Seth winced.

"Yes. This is our natural color. You will find a range here on earth." For the first time she spoke, keeping her voice even and calm.

The man turned to look at her again with a piercing gaze that had made her feel warm all over. "Truly?" His grin grew, and she found herself fascinated as the big alien lounged indolently in the chair. His vibrant blue eyes and silver-gray hair shone under the harsh lighting of the office. Instinct told her that she probably could trust him, but right now, she was feeling gun-shy. Being arrested again had been torture, and to find out they were to be charged with crimes against humanity had been enough to leave her reeling. Seth of course, had treated it like a huge joke, but she knew—after last time—there would be no quarter given.

"Why are you here?" Better to get these negotiations out of the way and hope it would give her some leverage to have them drop the charges.

"Our planet has lost an essential natural resource. Many *jahr* ago…"

"Jahr?" The unfamiliar and guttural word made no sense.

"Long periods of time. Used to denote the crop rotations passing."

Long time? Crop rotations passing? She searched through her head for a human alternative. "Umm… when the weather patterns change? Period of heat, then cool, then cold?" Maybe it was a season?

But he shook his head. "No. More than one set of weather patterns. Fiery sun, then cooler sun, then cool sun, then cold night, before it becomes warm once more."

Jessa cast her mind around. *Year? Could that be what he meant?* "Uh year? We have four seasons. One hot, one warm, then cold and back to warm? Then it starts again?"

He nodded.

Okay, that was a year or some similar measure of time. That was handy to know, but maybe they should set parameters for the language. "Seth, grab a notebook and we can write these words down with our translation."

OVER THE NEXT SEVERAL HOURS...OR *horanas* as Galan informed her, a glossary of terms emerged, allowing them to understand each other. Galan also engaged in a lightning quick exchange. He turned back to her. "I have informed my people to use your language where possible."

She smiled wanly. Holy hell. It was really happening. She was here in the middle of negotiations with...*an alien!*

From time to time, Chalmers checked in, bringing food and other items. At one stage, even a senior military officer ducked his head around the door. As he had every other time, Galan refused to deal with him, leaving the authorities frustrated, she was sure. She shivered each time she noted the angry glances they cast her way.

She wanted to say something, but her brain told her to control her mouth. At least for now, anyway. *They obviously think it's entirely my fault.* Not that it was, but there didn't seem much she could say to change their beliefs. *I'll be damned if I even try.* No one believed her last time, and she was sure they wouldn't this time either.

Occasionally Galan would look her way and her body's response was always the same. A long slow curl of interest, her mouth dried and her eyes searched his inscrutable face.

THE WOMAN REMAINED seated looking as if she were trying for anonymity, but each time he cast a glance at her, his reaction was instinctive and one he couldn't control. His fingers itched to trail over her fine skin. *So pale.* Her eyes were large in her face, and shining beacons to him. Her lips called to him on a primal level and he wondered if they were as soft and tender as they looked.

Galan wanted to close his lips over hers, to taste and feast upon her. Each time he gave in to the need to look at her, his body quickened, his groin tightened and the blood pumped through his veins faster. Not since the passing through the realms of his partner, Gospah, had he felt such a need to connect with another living being. To be with them on every level and that knowledge disturbed his equilibrium.

As time passed, he flagged and so did the humans sitting opposite him. *Horanas* had passed while they associated words, hoping to ease communications between them. He thanked his men for their thorough preparations prior to contact with the people of this planet, particularly monitoring and decoding their languages. Considering his next move, he caught the gaze of his personal guard, nodded then stood.

"I will retire for now, but it would be the greatest honor to have you join us this rest cycle." He watched intently as her face tightened. Something deep inside him told Galan that he must take this human to his ship and offer her protection. He'd always trusted his instincts before and right now they screamed that leaving her behind wasn't wise. That the anger of the ones who guarded them would boil over onto her.

The one called Seth stood up, knocking over his chair in his excitement. "Yeah, of course we will!"

Galan likened him to an overeager pet. He had to work hard to contain his amusement at the clumsy behavior, but he wasn't the one that Galan was concerned about. The woman watched him in silence as she had for *horanas.* She struck him as an intensely reserved creature, only sharing her thoughts when pushed hard. She seemed like someone who kept her counsel and emotions buried deep within her, but from time to time he caught glimpses of the vibrant nature she buried beneath the reserved façade.

Right now, her eyes glowed with interest and she slowly inclined her head. The movement unconsciously regal. *In a manner befitting a future consort of the king. Just as Gospah had always done. Do not bring Gospah into it,* he told himself, but he couldn't stem the thoughts. They already captured him.

"It would be my pleasure." Her voice, now husky with tiredness he assumed, stripped him emotionally. Galan knew then, that he would always protect this human. *This woman.*

"Come then. We will leave." He held out an arm and she looked at it, before reaching out trembling fingers. He gripped them, amazed to feel a charge shimmer through him.

The Quickening.

Galan inhaled unsteadily. Even with his beloved Gospah he had not felt that. The physical force of connection one made when finally touching their *Soul Partner.* He let his eyes close for just an instant, savoring the brief connection then opened them to see her watching him.

She wanted to ask what had just occurred; he could see it in the tremulous movement of her lips. But he knew she wouldn't. Not while Seth was there, in all likelihood. He nodded, and his men formed a physical barrier around the party of three then they left the room where they'd been contained.

As they exited the building, the one who'd challenged them earlier surged close. "You cannot take them with you." His face was angry, the mulish set of his chin and lips left Galan moderately amused and he fought to restrain himself.

"They will be my guests." Even as he spoke, his people continued to act as a shield as he inexorably drove them to his ship.

"You're not authorized…"

Jessa stepped up to the man, her face tight. "Oh, just can it would you?" Before she could say anything else, Galan moved between them, pulling her safely to his side.

"I don't *need* to be authorized. They are *my guests.*" Galan let just a hint of his anger show and the guard backed away nervously, eyes flicking from side to side.

As they stepped on to the eli-pad he released a sigh of relief as it rose into the ship. Then he turned to watch her face.

JESSA GASPED as the interior of the ship appeared. She didn't know what she had actually expected. Maybe the harsh white of the space ships in movies, but instead the welcoming yellows, pinks and minty greens soothed her. The alien, Galan, extended an arm. "Come this way." Her curiosity won her over as she followed him, his footsteps slow and measured and everywhere he went, others bowed deeply to him.

"What's your rank?" The suspicion that he was more than anyone guessed had risen throughout the hours of their meeting.

He grinned and the heat in her belly curled.

"An excellent question. My father is the liege lord of *Hesparia*." Everything about him warmed her, even as she absorbed who he was. He was the son of the planet's ruler? No wonder he had an air of command. "I am also Captain of this ship."

Jessa nodded silently. It made sense.

Seth continued bounding beside them, his head moving from side to side, while he peppered questions on the others who walked with them. Jessa let his excited chatter wash over her as they traversed what she was sure, was the length of the ship.

Galan seemed content to let her remain silent, and she was thankful. That little buzz she'd experienced when they touched had unsettled her. Together with knowing that when Galan left she'd be in deep trouble fed her uncertainty leaving her stomach churning and tossing.

Finally at the end of the long pastel hall he halted and pressed his hand against the wall. "Seth? This will be your chamber for the rest cycle." Jessa peered within as Seth entered. The room was large, spacious and calming, the walls glowing in muted tones of blue and green. A large bed lay in the center of the room and tinkling chimes piped through the air. A cursory goodnight came from Seth as he moved into the chamber.

A man, not quite as tall as Galan appeared at his shoulder. He didn't have the same commanding air, yet appeared comfortable with his position and level of authority.

"Joras, if you could ensure that Seth has everything he requires." The man called Joras bowed and Galan extended his hand, touching her briefly and once more the insistent buzz of connection shook her. Joras must have seen her step away quickly. He frowned at Galan who shook his head once.

"Come this way, Jessa." His voice was more of a caress.

Her mouth dried at the way it made her feel, like molten treacle invaded her limbs. He steered her to another point, then once again touched the wall. This time a much larger room opened before her. It was tinted in hues of pale mauve and blues. Jessa moved forward entranced. *So beautiful.* "It's perfect Galan!" She said swinging back to see his eyes watching her. A blush stained his cheeks.

"As are you, Jessa." He moved slowly, until he stood opposite her. His breath feathered over her sensitized skin. He raised a shaky hand to her cheek, and lightly caressed it. "As. Are. You." He leant in and their lips met. Her stomach quivered, and she couldn't ignore the reaction of her body and opened her mouth, welcoming the caress. Then he pulled away with a tiny smile and left her there.

Chapter 3

The muted lights from the night before slowly brightened as Jessa stretched lazily on the bed. After Galan had left, it had taken her ages to settle. The plush ablution room amazed her, fitted out with a softly rounded cleaning unit and even the toilet which warmed to skin temperature. When she had climbed into the bed it conformed to her body, cradling her as she drifted off and the lights had dimmed. If she didn't know better, Jessa would have thought the room read and adjusted to both her body temperature and heart rate.

With a sigh she rose, pulling the loose robe she had found around her body. It slipped over her naked skin and she sighed at the wickedly sensual pleasure it brought. A chime pealed and before she could answer the door slid open to let Galan in. Her heart rate increased. The kiss last night had been sensuous and soft and the room glowed subtly with shades of red and green—as it did right now. She carefully placed that information in her brain for discussion later.

"Good morning, Jessa." He bowed formally.

She returned it, realizing too late that the gown didn't close properly. His eyes gleamed but instead of the discomfort she would normally feel, it was replaced with the overwhelming question: What does he think of me? The red glow in the room increased.

"Umm, the room colour changes…?"

"It does. Depending on your emotions. The reaction of the body to stimuli." She blushed rosily.

An answering blush on his cheeks deepened and his eyes gleamed as he looked her over. With nerveless fingers, she pulled the gaping edges of the light robe together at her chest as reality set in. *He's an alien. One I've just met!*

He placed his fingers on her hand, the one still holding the robe closed, and she gasped at the intense reaction. "You honor me." His voice was deep and husky.

A secret thrill filled her.

"Soon…" He whispered the words close to her lips. She wanted to melt at the promise of ecstasy to come.

Jessa slid her hand free, then covered his fingers, savoring the supple warmth of his touch, the caress intimate. His fingers moved over the silky fabric covering her breast. Her breath caught, and she wobbled slightly from the intense emotions roiling within.

"Oh God…" The breathy words escaped and a shudder wracked her body.

In response, his slow movements stopped. "You do not… You do not wish this?"

His words died away. She looked at him, noting the grave expression on his face. For an instant she sensed his concern then it was gone. His eyes shuttered and the keen sense of loss startled her.

"No… Galan…" She reached out a hand but he shushed her.

"If you do not feel…"

"But I do. I feel it quite intensely. And it scares me."

His mouth quirked into a smile and the corners of his deep blue eyes crinkled.

"Then for you, we will slow down." He touched his lips to hers and the frisson of electricity shot through her as they softly opened. The movement was slight and slow, yet it stole her breath. Leaving her gasping in a sea of need while certain regions of her body nearly drowning in her desire.

She moved her fingers up his arms, grasping his shoulders. Firm and warm under her grip. Wide and strong, supporting her as her body sagged against his.

Leaning into him was a shock. Jessa really didn't know what she'd expected. The white tunic hadn't hinted at the strong and muscular chest she now sprawled against. Or the intense feeling of safety she'd found in his arms.

"Galan..." She whispered the words and he rumbled with laughter.

"I know."

"Not yet..." She winced, hearing the pleading tone in her voice.

"Soon, though. Very soon." Jessa closed her eyes.

WHILE THEY'D BROKEN their fast, Galan watched with wonder at the reactions and emotions which played over Jessa's face. He'd thought long and hard about the interaction between them in her cabin. How she'd interacted with him since they'd pulled apart. His body remained steeped in arousal. It plagued him during his rest cycle, so he experienced a new and unwelcome level of pain.

In the past, he'd have pleasured himself or taken the option of waiting until the feeling passed. Now it felt wrong to seek release in the former ways he'd practiced since Gospah's passing. With Gospah, his sex drive had been there, though far less than he experienced with Jessa. Now it had exploded into life, but only for this earthling. Suddenly he was dealing with a female who intrigued, aroused and yes, to be honest, teased his senses—albeit unknowingly—he was sure.

He and Jessa' had withdrawn from each other slowly and he ached at the loss of her warmth against him. Instead he waited while she retired to the ablution chamber to wash and dress before escorting her through the ship. Left alone with his thoughts and the memory of her soft body in his arms, the waiting had been difficult.

Their conversation once more returned to the cool and unemotional discussion of space travel and their respective languages during the meal. For the first time since the problem had arisen on his planet, hope filled him. Maybe, just maybe *he* might also find a partner. One who'd accept him as a man, not just the heir and one day ruler—something he feared above all. Perhaps he might talk Jessa into returning to his planet with him and she'd agree to partner him for the duration of their lives.

Confusion and concern warred with hopeful thoughts. How did he broach a problem like this? They needed the agreement of the ruling bodies on the planet. They couldn't just kidnap the women from here and drop them off on Hesparia, though that idea had been canvassed as an option, initially, by some of Hesparia's senators.

"How did you find out about us?" The words shook him from his introspective thoughts.

"We've known of this planet for hundreds of *jahrs*, once the truth of our history was rediscovered. It seems, millennia ago, the founders of our planet seeded a number of others with residents. In the early years, from what we've learned, there was ongoing communication between our planets, then something happened. We lost contact and with it, the communications skills and knowledge we shared."

He smiled, watching as she returned a small grin. The feeling of warmth filled him once more and his chest tightened. Now that he'd found the one who could be his partner, he needed to find a way to keep her.

"So, there's a reason you're here though, isn't there?" Seth voiced the question that concerned him.

How could he explain about the women? The need to rebuild the stocks of females it would take to fill the gene pool once more? The question he was sure could affect the outcome of any agreement between himself and Jessa.

They could have come much earlier, when the problem first came to notice. But there'd been barriers stopping them, he reminded himself grimly. They had only realized in the last few *jahr* that the inhabitants of earth had progressed sufficiently to allow them, under the terms of the United Galactic Treaty to be considered for contact.

"We have a problem. Our gene pool was seriously depleted some generations ago and our scientists sought ways to…" Galan breathed deeply, experiencing great difficulty in explaining. "They manipulated genes, which have degraded since the experimentation took place. At the time we were unaware what would occur. Our women are unable to sustain a full lifespan, because their genetic makeup is altered. They also cannot reproduce." Galan waited in silence for the response he expected.

Jessa looked horrified at his answer, her face flushed as she leaned in. "How could that possibly happen? What is wrong with letting life develop naturally?"

Galan nodded. "I agree. After that, we learned the importance of your words. Truly, if we could take back those actions, I know many of us would." He thought of the emotions he'd previously experienced, watching Gospah fade before his eyes. The pain and loss that plagued him had dimmed and the grief that had dragged at his mind like a fog on a valley floor leaving him unable to function clearly, slipped away.

She gripped his hand. "You lost someone close to you, didn't you, Galan?"

"My mother, my sister and…my partner. Gospah. Most of us here have. We've all felt the pain of loss."

Before retiring, Galan had removed the image of Gospah from the entry to his office. She'd remain a part of his past, but his future awaited him. He accepted it was time, without regret and prepared to seek a bright new life for himself, perhaps with this woman.

"I'm so sorry." He could see her surreptitiously clearing tears from her eyes with the tips of her fingers. "It must be hard for you." Her voice was husky, resulting in an unfamiliar tightening of his chest.

"It has been many yars… Is that right?" He struggled with the unfamiliar word.

A tiny burble of laughter erupted from between her lips. "Years. Many years." Jessa tugged away, placing her hand on the table. He laid one of his on top of hers, rubbing his thumb over her soft skin as she watched him. Her gaze questioning.

"Of course, that's not the only reason we made contact. We also desire allies."

Jessa smiled, pulling away. "Really? Why is that?"

He smiled back. "Small planet. Agrarian in nature."

Jessa wrinkled her nose and he felt captivation weave through him. It would be so very easy to lose himself in the web Jessa wove effortlessly. "Umm… should we go down and continue the negotiations? You really should meet with the officials."

"I would, but do you believe they will allow you to continue to participate?"

"Probably not." She let her eyes settle on his once more.

He shook his head. "Then that is not acceptable to me or my people." He sat back, the act regal and self-assured.

"Then how will we…?"

He smiled enigmatically as her words stopped short. "We tell them what we want. Then we wait."

THE DAYLIGHT HOURS PASSED SLOWLY, while communications moved back and forth between the ship and the single globally agreed point of contact. The Australian Prime Minister continued to insist on high level officials taking over the negotiations and Galan continued to refuse. The stalemate revolved around his desire for Jessa and Seth to take the lead role of intermediaries. In the meantime, Galan showed Jessa and Seth images of his homeland, giving them a crash course in the history of Hesparia. He tapped the rotating orb and it stilled in the air.

"This is the main continent, Orsar. It is the center of trade and commerce as well as where I and my family live."

"Really? Can we see your home?" Seth was eager but at his words, Jessa could see the darkening of Galan's eyes.

An instant of disorientation filled her then the seed of fear grew in her chest. "Galan?" But instead of answering, Galan turned away.

"Not now." The fear of what he hid warred with any positive emotions she experienced. Ones that told her he meant no harm. *How do you know that?* Her brain demanded answers she couldn't possibly provide. She let her eyes catch Seth's and saw for the first time the hint of fear in his too. But unlike Seth, she was no puppy, blindly following. Now was the time to make a stand.

"Galan, we need to return to our homes and families." Jessa said the words carefully but with intent.

"No."

The words filled her with concern. *He's holding us prisoner here?* "Galan? We have families who'll be worried about us. We have lives…" Turning carefully to search his face she could see a cold implacability there.

"No. I won't let you go. You can make contact with your families, I am sure. Once this is settled."

Seth rose, jerking her attention back to him. "Now… mate, you can't keep us here. We're Aussies…" His words were forced, as if he too had just come to the conclusion of their status as prisoners. Jessa wanted to laugh at the look on his face, but the situation was less than funny.

One more time. She had to try one more time. "Galan, you haven't told us why you are here, but if you don't let us go, they'll likely see you as a threat. You need to release us."

"Why? Because I won't show you where I live?" The angry tones stopped Jessa. "My father rules Hesparia—the whole planet. That is what I didn't wish to raise with you. Satisfied now?"

"Not really. If your father rules Hesparia, then why are you here?" She already knew about some of the difficulties, the problem with the women and children… But surely not? Her mind scrambled wildly. She took a deep breath, settling her wild conjectures. She needed to know that they—Seth and herself—hadn't made the worst decision of what could, potentially, be their short lives.

"Because we need women. Women happy to travel to Hesparia. To take partners and to bear children."

The stark words stole her breath. *Dear stars in heaven.* The situation was worse than anything she could've imagined. Not once, even though he'd told her about the issue of women on Hesparia had she even considered this possible outcome.

"But... We may not even *be* compatible!" The words erupted.

He laughed, harshly. "We are. Generations ago, our people and yours were the same. Our people were deposited on the planets in order to populate them. Seeded if you like. But the ones who brought us here, the other species, are ones we have long since lost contact with. But our scans... They've told us that we remain compatible.

"This is the first time, since then, that we have made contact with your people. Among us were technicians and educators. They kept their knowledge alive. The knowledge of travel, ships and language were documented and saved. They were studied by the greatest minds on our planet. Our shared history means that your genetic material and ours are more than compatible."

The harsh words sat Jessa on her backside in the chair. *Dear heavens.* The Hesparians wanted breeders. And she had been the first to enter. What did that mean for her? For humanity?

GALAN KNEW he'd frightened her. It was clear in the pallor of her face and the way she carefully avoided touching him. Her moving away each time he stepped near her angered him.

It wasn't what he'd planned, but at this point, he also couldn't call back his words. They'd been said. In trying to keep his own true identity hidden, he'd damaged the fragile connection growing between them, leaving him frustrated and on edge.

He hadn't even had a chance to explain about the other aspect of their mission. No. She needed to know, but perhaps he should focus on dealing with this first?

Negative emotions welled as she perched beside Seth, silently watching him. The growing need to reach out and soothe the look on her face tore at every fiber of his being.

"They have agreed." Joras called out to him and Galan didn't know if he felt relief that this part of the stalemate with the government of Earth was over, or frustration that Jessa would leave the ship soon.

That he could no longer request her presence made him want to rage. Irritation coursed and the unfamiliar emotion angered him.

With Gospah there'd been no need to command her obedience, she'd been naturally easy going. Truly, he didn't even think that would have been what he wanted, anyway.

"Fine." He couldn't give more than a single word answer. To do so would push him too far and he was sure his temper would snap, leaving him reacting in a forceful manner which would push Jessa further away.

Galan turned and left the room, but as the door sealed behind him he castigated himself for his foolish behavior. He'd only known her for such a short period of time. Maybe he was wrong about the *Quickening* too.

"Galan?" Galan knew of Joras' concern that something was afoot. Perhaps it was because they had been serving together for so long, that they knew each other's action and reactions.

But that wasn't right. He'd been acting wrong since the moment he'd met Jessa.

"Joras, I don't think I can…" He sucked in an unsteady breath, staring sightlessly at the wall opposite.

"You have to let her go. At least for now." Joras touched his shoulder and the urge to throw it off raged for an instant. It swelled, and Galan tensed, fighting off the feeling.

"I know." Saying the words acknowledged the pain filling his body. Let go of his partner? The one he'd experienced the *Quickening* with? If that was actually what had happened, his mind added. Letting her go was wrong, in every way. His muscles coiled tight with anguish.

He dragged in an unsteady breath and then another, attempting to push the pain away. "You have to do it now." Joras muttered but Galan knew that Joras understood his pain.

"Escort them out." His gut churned and his voice was low and harsh. He knew, if he had to escort Seth and Jessa out himself, he wouldn't be able to let her go. The primal directive of holding onto a partner too strong to overcome. "Take over the negotiations." He whispered the words, passing Joras the small information cube. "This is the information we currently have." With that, he willed his legs to move, carrying him down the long corridor to his office. Each step away from her caused a new layer of pain so that by the time he'd found his seat he shivered and shook under the strain. It was too much. He couldn't let Jessa go.

JORAS, Galan's second, returned to the room where they'd waited. His careful behavior agitated Jessa as she watched him in the growing silence, remaining on the seat where she sat, fingers twined around each other. It was a vain hope that she could contain her inner struggle. Seth moved closer to her, as if sensing the silent dispute that carried on within her and she was thankful he held his counsel. She didn't want to attempt any kind of normal conversation right now.

On one level, there was the fear of the unknown. After all, what did she know about Galan and his intentions? On the other, there was a connection she couldn't explain between them. Knowing that Galan had left her here, in this anonymous room with Joras hurt. She ached internally, in a way she had never before experienced. A feeling she didn't want to experience any time soon and that increased her sense of confusion.

No matter, Jessa told herself, she was a realist. She tried vainly to shrug off the hurt and confusion, while she let her brain search for explanations to her current state. Maybe it was some weird form of Stockholm Syndrome? Jessa nearly laughed out loud at the thought, but deep down, even that didn't exactly describe the emotions running through her.

"We need to go out now." Joras' voice dragged Jessa from her internal dialogue and she stood, turning briefly to see if Galan was in sight as they left the room. But he was nowhere to be seen in the long pastel colored corridor and her heart sank.

"Galan isn't coming?" How bitterly she wanted to call the words back as Joras smiled at her. It was a sympathetic movement, making her feel as if her feelings were transparent. Something she didn't want to happen.

"No. He has tasks to complete." His words were kind, but left Jessa with no doubt that the conversation revolving around Galan was now closed. With that, Jessa and Seth were hastened to the small elevator area they'd entered the ship through. The moving pad was steady beneath their feet as they boarded it and Jessa promised herself, she wouldn't look back. Instead she locked her knees and looked determinedly forward, ignoring the crushing pain growing in her chest. Every step and move exacerbating the situation in a way she couldn't understand. As if there were an unseen otherworldly tether between Galan and herself.

On reaching the ground they stepped up to be met by a crowd of armed personnel, demanding that she and Seth step toward them. Jessa looked around, trying to understand what was happening. They'd willingly exited the ship, so what caused this? She stepped closer, slightly confused.

Jessa felt a brutal hand extend through the barrier of guards. She cried out, feeling the harsh bite of the grip on her wrist. The pressure hurtful and she tried to pull away in fright.

At her cry, a pushing and shoving war erupted between the Hesparians and humans. Jessa struggled against the hold that bit cruelly into her flesh, even as she reached out for the small knot of Hesparians with her other hand. To her dismay, they'd begun retreating back to the ship, leaving her lost in the seething morass of bodies.

Seth looking back at her from the circle of guards. His mouth moved but in the middle of the boiling confrontation his words were lost. She noted his distress even as she jerked against the tether.

Voices continued to babble around her, but there were too many, drowning each other out so no one direction was clear enough for her to understand, among the yelling combatants.

She twitched and turned, pulled and pushed, attempting to escape.

Finally, Jessa managed to wrench herself away from the restraining clasp. "Wait!"

Her shriek was ignored as another action knocked her back to the human camp. A shove from behind left her balance precarious and the final stomp of a foot on hers resulted in a fall to the wet trampled grass.

A body tripped over her, and pain radiated through her leg, stealing her breath. Another fell over them crushing her further and the sounds changed, swelling as a hard object hit the back of her head and darkness grew around her. Jessa closed her eyes, letting the welcome blackness swallow her.

GALAN QUICKLY DEPRESSED the communications button, hoping to contact Joras before he exited the craft, ready to demand he wait, but it was too late. The thought of her being unable to contact him flashed through his mind as he remembered the item he'd planned to give her. He quickly patted his pants. The small communication device he'd meant to give remained in his pocket. *How could I have overlooked that?*

He pressed the button to engage the viewer, only to see his worst nightmare taking place. Joras being pushed back to the ship and Jessa—his beautiful Jessa—pulled forcibly from within their protective circle. His people worked to ensure Joras' safety before Jessa's. She fell, lost in the mêlée and he shuddered, gut churning at the horrifying sight.

"No!"

He rose unsteadily and rushed through the doorway, then down the corridor. Heart thumping wildly. He couldn't lose Jessa. Not now!

Joras and the security detail had returned to the ship, as Galan made it to the room with the eli-pad. "What happened? We need to send men…"

Joras laid a calm hand upon his arm and Galan wanted to pull away. "We have Seth still. We have leverage."

But the words scoured Galan. "No." He pushed forward, then surprise filled him as Joras clasped him, forcing him to stop.

"Now is not the time."

Joras' words aggravated Galan but he pushed the emotion aside. The connection he felt with Jessa swelled, stealing his breath then was abruptly cut off. He shuddered. "Something is wrong. Something has happened." He looked into Joras' face. "I can't feel her anymore."

Joras inhaled sharply. "What do you mean...you can't feel her? You haven't...? She isn't...?"

Galan's stomach churned and right then he didn't care who knew it. "I felt the *Quickening*." He released the tension in his body. "Something happened and I can't feel her anymore."

"We'll get her Galan." He heard the words and saw Seth's face. It was white and strained at the shock of his bald announcement. Unable to focus his gaze, Galan knew he had to pull himself together. His compatriots needed him to make good strong decisions that for their future. They relied on his actions to save their home world. To forge alliances. To *be* their future.

With a deep but unsteady breath, Galan pulled free of Joras. "You're right. We must plan. Especially if we intend to bring back enough women and manage some form of diplomatic alliance after this mess." He kept his eyes on the wall. He'd already shared enough of the fear with his crew to leave them wondering about his mental stability. Another shuddering breath and he held himself still. "We'll retire to my office." He turned on a heel. "Ensure Seth has appropriate care and meet me there." Long, purposeful strides took him to his ward room, he slumped into his seat.

His eyes sought the video feed watching the humans as they milled around. Their military remained on watch outside the ship and the frustration and anger churned through him again. He couldn't see any sign of Jessa now, and he closed his eyes.

WHEN JESSA WOKE, there was light, sound and acute discomfort radiated down her left leg. The groggy feeling remained, but she opened her eyes. A hospital—she was in a hospital bed, and her heart began the slow rhythmic ache that had begun when she left Galan. *How long ago had that been?*

She turned her head. *A private room.* Something was definitely wrong with this story, she told herself. Why would she be in a private room in a hospital? Memories of the scene outside the ship blasted into her mind. Someone had fallen on her. Actually, more than one, if she didn't mistake it. The awful crushing feeling, and the pain in her leg.

Bip Bip Bip. The beeping she hadn't noticed until now sped up, annoying Jessa.

The door opened silently and a large woman, dressed in hospital scrubs entered. "Awake finally. Good to see." She moved with a ruthless efficiency, whipping a thermometer out before popping it into Jessa's ear.

"How long have I…?"

"Been here? Two and a half days." The nurse held her hand up and waited for the piercing sound. "No temp. Good."

"Where am I?" Jessa wasn't all that sure she really did want to know. But she'd learned not to ignore something scary.

"In Parkes Community Hospital. Why?"

Jessa blinked. *In Parkes?* So, it wasn't the jail hospital. That made her feel a little easier. "But… I'm in a private room?" *Damn.* She didn't have any health insurance. This was going to cost. It would really damage her bank account. It would likely be way more than she had to her name. Perhaps she could sell her story to a woman's magazine? The idle thought left her wanting to laugh hysterically.

"Yes. The Government apparently is picking up the tab, or at least so I heard. Now, let's sit you up a little." The nurse lifted a hand-held device tethered to the bed and the end rose, sitting her up. "The doctor will be here soon to do rounds. You're going to want to look at least semi presentable for that."

The nurse reached for the small table beside the bed, grabbed the cheap brush and handed it over. "You'll also want to clean up. I'll send one of the girls in to help you in a minute."

She turned, her shoes squeaking on the linoleum floor and headed for the door before throwing a final instruction over her shoulder. "Now be a good girl and get ready."

The door swung shut behind her ample bulk and Jessa was alone once more.

Chapter 4

Galan paced. Joras had contacted the Government, stating their concern for Jessa. They'd been stonewalled. No one wanted to tell him her condition. Each small infraction increased his frustration until he was ready to erupt. The cloak of anger closing around him. Seth shared what he'd seen, leaving Galan feeling overcome with churning emotions—rage, frustration and a deep well of fear. In the last few hours, something had changed. He could feel her once more, though his body ached as never before and his chest constricted.

Obviously she'd woken, which relieved him but the physical distance between them was insupportable. He scowled. *What more can we do to get Jessa back to the ship, where she belongs?* He paced the room again, aware that Joras watched with concerned eyes. "Galan, we can offer our healing services."

Galan stopped. Still and silent, willing Joras to continue while his beleaguered mind whirred back to life. "We could couch it as a gesture of goodwill. Well done, Joras."

It wouldn't be enough he knew, but better than the distance between them now.

Once Jessa was healed, he'd once more refuse to deal with the humans unless Jessa was involved. That cheered him a little, dulling the pain of separation. "Do it."

With a silent bow, Joras headed to the door. But just as he reached for the palm screen, he stopped. "They might refuse."

Galan had already come to that conclusion. "They could, but we can sweeten the deal a little. Improve the odds in our favor."

Joras watched him silently until the awareness dawned on him. "Ahh, we could offer healing to some others. Some who are beyond the ability of their own healers?"

Galan inclined his head. Whatever it took, to get Jessa back to him.

With a whoosh of the door Joras was gone, leaving Galan by himself in his office. He sat heavily in the chair, waiting for the reply. It would take time, he knew, but he had to try everything now.

After what felt like *horanas*, he rose and headed to the door just as it cracked open. Joras stood on the other side, his face pale.

"What? What has happened?"

"They have agreed on certain conditions." He waited quietly. Not answering the first, and to Galan's mind, the most important question of all.

"What conditions?" His body locked tight with anger. *They had no right...* He stopped his thoughts right there. Of course they did. They were the government of this planet. But he didn't and wouldn't like it. Not one bit.

"They have a number of inoperable tumor sufferers and some other diseases. One called something odd... I can't remember the term."

Galan urged him on in silence. Uncaring of the suffering of others for now, as his body and mind demanded answers. He just needed to know the status of Jessa and willed Joras to share the knowledge. But Joras continued to look at him a strange and fearful expression on his face. "What?"

"She has been bodily damaged."

The air was sucked from his lungs. He reached blindly for the door jam. "Bodily damaged? How and where?" He heard his own voice, the rasp of his demand though the haze of devastated emotions.

"They won't release details. Just that she is under a healer's care and the injury will take a long time to repair. Longer than we have here."

"Take them all. Whatever we must do. But get her back to us." He stopped and gulped convulsively. "She is important to me."

Joras nodded in silence and beat a retreat.

JESSA HAD JUST ABOUT HAD ENOUGH. LOCKED in the small hospital room in a cast was not her idea of a great time. Of course, since she had been here, all sorts of government types had come and hounded her. How had she managed to make contact? What other species had they heard from? Each time her answers were the same. It wasn't me, I didn't do it. I can't help you.

Each time felt worse than the last and she rubbed her chest in an unconscious action before realizing what she'd done. Of course, it did no good. The pain continued and the doctors had been unable to find a medical reason for the constant ache deep in her chest.

Three quick raps sounded, and Jessa cocked her head. Her parents had come and gone just that morning. She wasn't expecting anyone else, so who could it be? "Come in."

The door swung open to admit the head of the hastily convened security service. "Miss Bankia? Jessa?" He smiled, and Jessa could just about count his perfectly capped teeth in the well-practiced look.

"Inspector Verdain, I presume? I've been over all this before."

He held up a quick hand. "No. There's been a breakthrough."

She sucked in a breath and held it. *A breakthrough?*

"The captain has offered the services of his healer. In exchange, we've managed to get some inoperable patients an opportunity for help."

"And?" Her voice was tense in the quiet room.

"Then you can return home."

"Not good enough." She yelled, and he winced. "I want back into the negotiations."

He shook his head. "I'm sorry…"

"I don't care about sorry. Just get me back there."

"Look…. I'm only here to let you know they've offered to heal you. Nothing more than that."

Jessa stilled. Offered to heal her? He'd kissed her. Perhaps it meant… "Find out about the negotiations. I want to be involved.

The man blushed, and she was sure there was a fair dose of rage involved. Her parents had already told her she was too demanding. But she refused to be locked out.

He moved away, dialed a number on his cell phone and started talking to someone in low tones. Ones she couldn't make out, but the slump in his shoulders at the end and the sigh knotted her stomach once more.

"All right. They've agreed to that."

"Excellent." Then his previous words impinged. "And?" She demanded, leaning closer to the man before her. "How does this affect me?"

"He's insistent that you be seen by their healer first. They seem to think they can somehow speed up the healing process."

He'd done a deal. It didn't matter why. Others would benefit, she reminded herself. "Okay. What do I need to do?"

"I'll send in a nurse to ensure you're dressed. We'll leave as soon as you're ready. They refuse to see any of other patients until you're there."

"All right then." The agent smiled again, and once more the man made her stomach pitch and churn. "Wait! Did they mention Seth?"

The agent smiled over his shoulder, reaching for the handle of the door. "Yes. He'll be there too." With that he heaved the door open and entered the corridor beyond. Jessa waited for the sound of his footsteps to die away as excitement mounted. The reality of his reasons came back to her with a rush.

They needed breeders.

But in the back of her mind, a little whisper irritated: What if he wanted something different? More? What if that was just one part of the story? She snorted at the fanciful notion as the nurse sailed into the room.

"They told me you're being released into the care of the government. I'm not sure I like this." The woman muttered the words as she bustled around, raising the bed and dropping Jessa's foot from the sling. "Normally we'd keep you a little longer…"

Jessa let the woman mutter while she stripped out of the bed clothes, hauling on the blouse and skirt she'd worn in the accident. At least they weren't jeans, she thought with a giggle.

The nurse looked up. "Are you okay?" Her tone and face suspicious and Jessa schooled herself back to her usual calm exterior. "Yeah."

Once dressed, the nurse gave her a crash course using crutches, making her do circuits of the room before she declared herself satisfied. After everything was packed into the small overnight case her parents had brought with them, a wheelchair was trundled in for Jessa. Her purple cast stuck out from under the light floral material of her skirt.

The agent returned and pushed her down the hall to the waiting car. He and an orderly settled her into the back seat of the SUV. He checked her seatbelt was in place before they rolled down the drive. Flashes of light caught Jessa unaware and she turned, noting the knot of bodies holding cameras and microphones. "What's going on?"

"Everyone wants to know about Jessa Bankia. Why she was able to make first contact and what happened after a night on the spaceship."

The drive through the streets was uneventful and soon they turned off to the access road. Another knot of people waited, but this time some carried placards with phrases such as *"Aliens Don't Believe In God"* and *"Don't Trust the Aliens. We Don't Know Why They Are Here"* emblazoned across them. Jessa gulped. "Have they been here long?"

The agent smothered a laugh. "Ever since your friends arrived."

She squirmed in her seat looking beyond the shrubbery, now

that they had cleared the security post. *There*. In the distance she could finally see the ship. Her chest loosened, and the curious pain that had been there began to disappear.

A line of ambulances waited outside the building and they drove closer, slowly. "They wish to see you before they begin treatments. So, we're going to take you into the building. You'll be guarded at all times, you have no reason to fear what will happen."

Jessa wanted to scream that they hadn't hurt her. That it was the humans, but the words stuck in her throat. Instead, she nodded mutely.

HE HEARD A VEHICLE APPROACH. For the last hour, he struggled to remember to use their terms, all the while impatiently waiting for the appointed time to arrive. Joras was calm and patient, something Galan had always considered himself to be. Until today.

The rumble of voices intruded on his internal ruminations. *Is it her? Is she truly here?* Each time he'd heard one of their land-based vehicles he'd stood, waiting only to have his hopes dashed as another ailing and sickly human entered the room. The ache in his chest released a little more.

The door opened and there she stood. Pale, sweating and obviously in pain. He didn't dash to her side, even though his body demanded it. He had to act nonchalant. Joras had hammered that home, and he knew, on a purely subconscious level, that was the advice he would have given to anyone in his position. But this time, he struggled to remain impassive.

He scanned her with his gaze, taking in the wooden aides under her arms. He checked her over, dipping to her breasts, full and high beneath her light top and down to the skirt. Finally, he caught sight of the monstrosity on her leg. Bodily damaged, Joras had reported. Rage grew, contorting within him like an angry dragon ready to soar. With ruthless efficiency he chained it.

Jessa hobbled her way to a chair. He moved, dragging out a seat and watched as she settled into it with a grateful grunt. The agent at his side pulled another chair up and slowly raised the leg to the padded surface. She hissed and Galan curled his fingers into the flesh of his palms. "Jessa? What happened to you?"

She turned and he could see the pain dazing her eyes.

"Healer? Deal with Jessa first." He bit the words out. Waiting as his medics came closer, scanning her body with a small portable device before shaking their head.

"Barbarians." He could hear the healer's comments and agreed inwardly with the sentiment. In a flash the man was crossed the room, sifting and sorting through his assortment of technology and herb-based remedies. Satisfied, he came back and attempted to gain access to the leg. "How do you get to the flesh with this stuff all over it?"

Once more Galan watched as the medic hustled back to Jessa, the whole time fury bubbled below the surface. *How could this have happened to my Jessa?* He returned with a small sonic cutter and made a careful incision in the dried paste on her leg. Jessa winced and looked away and for the first time since she had returned to him, Galan could see the damage wrought on her body. The bruises and pain lines bracketing her mouth.

Once the material had been cut away and an access point created in the cast, he could see the purple and swollen flesh below. He retreated a little way, refusing to empty his stomach before her.

Her pain-filled whispers forced him to turn around, and he waited while his gut clenched. The healer held a small bone regenerator against her skin. Galan reached out and she gripped his hand tight, squeezing. He accepted the pain, hoping to offer her some support during the process of her bone set and regrew around the obvious fracture. Finally, her grip loosened and her face began to lose the white pinched look.

The man sighed. "How do we even get this thing off?"

The agent moved in. One of Galan's security detail stopped him.

With a small grunt the medic inspected the purple mass, retreated to his bag and hunted noisily. When he returned, he held a larger cutter and slid it against the cast as Jessa named it, until the front section fell away. Galan held his breath, watching the medic at work, knowing one slip and her skin would be cut too. Then he instructed Jessa to stand in a gruff voice.

Jessa's eyes caught his, and he could read the fear and trepidation in their depths. With an inhaled breath she reached for the aids, but the physician tut tutted and shook his head. "You won't need them."

Galan extended a hand and she stood, placing the injured leg on the floor, gingerly "Oh. My. God." He smiled at the comment. "You fixed me!" She let go of Galan and flung both arms around the healer with a squeal.

The other man looked at Galan, a horrified expression filling his face and tried to disentangle himself while Galan guffawed at her reaction. "Come now, Jessa. Let the healer do his job."

She looked at him and smiled, placing her fingers back in his. He savored the strength of her grip and the connection between them. Her breath caught, her eyes sparkled and her cheeks regained a pink glow. It stopped him in his tracks as his mouth dried.

I won't be able to let her go. Ever. The thought crashed into him as the agent stepped up to them.

JESSA TOOK a step closer to Galan, the amazement at her recovery now overshadowed by anger in the face of the agent who stood before them. Not that she honestly thought that he would hurt her, but something deep and primal told her she needed to stay close to Galan.

The agent must have seen something in either her or Galan's face and he stopped. Galan's security officer waited, his shoulders hunched as if ready to act. Jessa inched against Galan who wrapped an arm around her.

"Come. We have work to do."

Jessa looked up at him in amazement. *Here I am in the middle of the room, with people watching me. What am I doing?* Immediately she pulled away and heard him snicker.

"This way." He indicated through a small doorway where a table sat and there at the end was Seth.

He smiled broadly on seeing her. She grinned back and made her way to the empty seat beside him. It wouldn't do to embarrass herself further, she thought ruefully.

Once they took their places, she noted Joras, Galan, herself and Seth were joined by two others. She looked at Seth.

He shrugged. "I don't know who they are."

A pen and pad waited on the table and she gratefully clutched them, cleared her throat and asked, "So, do we take minutes? And do we know everyone at the table? I don't know these gentlemen."

They both turned to stare at her. She wanted to shrink under their silent searching and slightly intimidating gazes.

The older man, wearing spectacles and a suit, cleared his throat. "I'm here on behalf of the Prime Minister."

Jessa waited, looking at him.

He stared back.

"Oh, for heaven's sake. What is your name for the record?"

He leaned back and made a steeple with his hands. "My name is Dr. Lovejoy. And I am still unaware of how you came to be involved in these negotiations, Miss Bankia?" His haughty tone and steely gaze were no doubt, supposed to make her feel inferior, but a burble of laughter rose in her chest.

Jessa coughed to cover the snorting sound that escaped and formed a small fist with her hand. "Because I am. That's all you need to know right now." She grinned, satisfied at the shocked look on his face. "And the man next to you?" She settled once more, the fingers of her other hand cramping as she gripped the pen tightly. She ran the nail of her thumb along the smooth surface.

"Rear Admiral Denton."

Jessa nodded and jotted down the names. "Right, so where do we begin?"

Galan caught her eye and she noticed the furtive wink he sent her way. Seth kicked her foot under the table, hard and Jessa had to stop the 'oww' from escaping.

The meeting progressed slowly. The government pressed for the removal of Seth and Jessa from the working party, Galan blocked it effectively, his voice firm each time it was raised. In the first hours Joras said little as did Seth and Jessa. The government wanted access to their medical systems. Galan smiled, making a sound of non-committal agreement and Jessa smothered a giggle at the dance of politics which continued around her.

They broke after three hours and the two suited men left. Galan released a breath and sat back down after escorting them to the door. "Now we can begin our discussions properly."

Surprise filled Jessa as she whipped around. "What do you mean?"

"They were not here as members of the official discussion, Jessa. Didn't they tell you anything while your healers attended to you?"

Jessa shook her head, the swish of hair around her head forming a red curtain. "No. What should I have known?"

"In order to continue the negotiations on this level, we offered to treat a finite number of patients for illnesses and diseases that your own healers had no treatment for."

She touched her cheeks, feeling the flame. *He's done this for me?* Then her skin cooled as she turned away from his face, her belly churning. *What does he want from me?* But she already knew. He wanted her body. *To breed children and help repopulate his world.* The thought, unbidden flashed through her mind. Bitter bile rose in her throat. *Surely, he wants more from me?* But she wouldn't allow herself to be fooled into thinking that she was any more than a means to an end.

She'd already learned that lesson once. And it had cost her, dearly.

"Fine. Then let's get busy." She kept her voice business like, taking her seat once more and noted the frown on the faces of the men before her. Galan watched, clearly puzzled before he gave a short nod and sat down opposite her.

HE SCRUTINIZED. Somewhere between the two men leaving and

them sitting down, he'd either done or said something that had changed her mind about him once again. For the life of him, though, he couldn't work out what it had been and his temper frayed around the edges. Now Jessa sat opposite him, focused on finding some kind of agreement where he could talk to their heads of state. The whole time, her persona was cold and remote. Frustration filled him, winding his nerves tighter.

"Fine. I'll ask for a teleconference call. We can patch in the Prime Minister and their office can arrange a venue you find suitable." She wrote the note on the pad then stood. "I'll go and request that right now." Her movements still a little jerky, as if she expected her leg to buckle under her weight, slight though it was.

Joras laid a comforting hand on his arm. "It grows late, and we must return to the ship. Now would be a perfect time to make that request."

He nearly rolled his eyes at Joras, but knew what he meant. "Jessa, we need to return to our ship. You and Seth would be more than welcome to join us."

She turned and he could see the indecision on her face. "Well, I don't..."

"What if we leave and they don't let us back into the negotiations?" Seth wheedled.

Galan wanted to thank the small man opposite him. But that would only anger Jessa. And right now he needed to rebuild the bridge between them that he'd destroyed somehow.

She vacillated. Then nodded. "Of course you're probably right, Seth."

Jessa opened the door, spoke briefly in whispers to the man beyond and closed it again. "Right then, we should go to your ship, immediately and reconvene at...say, nine a.m.?"

"Of course." He acceded.

They trooped out the door and he noticed that a different male agent slipped into the entourage behind Jessa. Joras would take care of that, or his men, anyway, he thought. Thankful she'd at least decided that the offer was no more than indicated. At this point, anyway.

The security detail folded in around them as they headed for the ship. They had been informed that overnight, the requested conference technology would be installed and the Prime Minister would be involved in the next round of talks via this communication system.

Jessa and Seth would continue acting as the go between for the two races. She accepted the responsibilities heaped upon her as stoically as possible. He watched the way her brows creased and how she thought carefully before answering any questions. It was something he doubted Seth understood or grasped the importance of as he chattered away happily. All those things would come in time, Galan reminded himself. Seth was still young and he wondered at the age of his Jessa. She looked young yet she carried herself with a dignity many older women could only wish for.

Jessa moved close by his side, and he was reminded by the scene he'd watched on the viewer, when she'd been hurt. The security team were thoroughly briefed this time: Jessa was to be afforded the privileges of one of the crew, but in his mind, it seemed more important than ever that she not be spooked with that knowledge. Not yet. He would make sure she knew when the time was right. When he'd made the announcement, there'd been some odd looks, before everyone agreed to his plan. He didn't know what Joras had told them afterward, but they accepted the direction without comment—at least to his face.

This time, she was kept to the center of the group and Galan grasped her hand firmly. Her fingers trembled slightly, unable to miss the sound of distant chanting and shouting.

"Damn protestors." He heard the words from the agent behind him. Jessa shook harder. He increased the pace of his footsteps.

The agent moved closer.

Galan spared him a glance, slipped his arm around Jessa and hurried her along.

The crowd grew louder, some of the voices tinny as they shoved against the barriers. The sea of people undulated as Jessa, Galan and the detail finally arrived at the eli-pad. They formed a circle on the metallic floor and started ascending just as bodies broke through the fencing. The crowd ran in the direction of the ship, but he and his people were too high for even the most athletic to reach them.

The eli-pad engaged with the ship and Galan let out a pent up breath. Jessa shuddered in his arms.

He turned to his second. "Joras, deal with him," he pointed to the agent. "And do whatever you must to get rid of *them*." He directed Joras' attention to the scene below the eli-pad.

Joras would know what he meant, but right now, his concern was for Jessa. Carefully he steered her away from the rest of the party and to the cabin she'd stayed in before.

The door opened and he led her inside before pulling her into his arms. She hadn't spoken a word and that concerned him. "Jessa?"

She shivered and shook in his careful embrace and he cursed. Then slowly, he pulled her tighter against him. Wanting only to take in her pain, but the moment their bodies touched, his fired with need. A current surged between them and she lifted her eyes. "Galan?" Her words a mere whisper that he strained to hear. "Could you… Would you stay?" She gulped, and his chest heated, as did the rest of his body. "Will you stay with me tonight?"

AN ICY CHILL had taken control of Jessa's body the moment the crowd had started chanting. Visions of the altercation where she'd been injured made her fearful. Jessa clung to Galan as a safe harbor in the maelstrom. Even when they were safe aboard the ship, she'd been unable to throw off the fear. Instead it roiled within like some whirling dervish.

Galan escorted her to the cabin and she'd relaxed a little, though she still shook from the stress and fright, and she shivered. Her body demanded the reassurance that only he could give, while her brain entered a whole new twilight zone. His presence comforted her, impressing her with the sense of safety and security. The nightmare she'd lived through in the hospital was bad enough, but she feared her nightmares would be worse after seeing the protestors.

Her mouth engaged before her brain considered the ramifications of the question and she'd asked him to stay the night. What on earth had possessed her?

But now, here he was—smiling at her in his enigmatic fashion. She took in the silver-gray hair, the muscular and incredibly toned body hidden under his shapeless coverall and the heat of him. His piercing blue eyes promised depths she wanted to fall into. The hard planes of his face were inscrutable and she held her breath as he advanced. He towered over her. Her stomach pitched and yawed as barely suppressed emotions swamped her.

Does he want to…sleep with me? She couldn't stop the thought and her knees no longer wanted to hold her upright. Blindly Jessa groped for the bed and sat heavily, the breath rushing from her lungs with a loud sigh.

"Do you wish to talk?" His voice was warm, and she melted a little more. He moved again, making a spot beside her on the bed before sitting down. His actions rolled her close to him. The scent of him, masculine and somehow piney, filled her senses. Just as she was ready to reach out and grasp his shoulders to haul him closer, he moved. *What the…?* Her beleaguered brain couldn't easily compute as a rush of sexual arousal filled her. *Why has he moved away?*

She looked up at his implacable face. "So, what would you like to discuss?" His words were cold and distant, but the tic at his cheek told her he wasn't as unaffected as he made out. The tension seeped from her body as she looked at his hands, tightly curled into a hard-cold fists, the way the muscles in his legs strained beneath the fabric of his pants and the bulge that she was sure she could detect. *No. He definitely wasn't unaffected.*

"Do we…do we have to talk?" She whispered the words, watching him shut his eyes and shame filled her. Neither of them was sure of the other and her request obviously made him very uncomfortable. She sighed. "Look, if you want… I'll be…" Jessa gulped on the words as they stuck in her throat. "I'll be fine." She turned away, hoping he wouldn't see the truth in her eyes. Of course, she wouldn't be fine, but she could survive tonight. And every other one that came after.

A gentle hand touched her shoulder. "No. I will stay with you. Watch over you."

His words left her ready to weep. No one had ever been there just for her. Giving her the support she so desperately needed, without seeing something in it for them. Her eyes burned and the moisture in her throat dried up.

"Thank you." Jessa struggled with her emotions, not turning around until she was sure she wouldn't fall on him in a weeping mess. But when she did finally turn back to Galan, she could see the concern clear in his eyes.

"Better now?"

He knew. Darn him. She'd tried so hard to hide her emotions.

"Go prepare for your rest. I will wait here."

She left him, retreating to the bathroom in silence, leaving him sitting there on the bed.

SHE SLEPT SOUNDLY, curled into his arms and he ached with unfulfilled arousal. Since she'd emerged from the bathing room, quiet and somewhat withdrawn, he'd watched her. She was like a ticking bomb to him. Any moment, he could expect another outpouring of sensual torture. *No. That's not right. She doesn't do it consciously.* He remembered how she'd made her way to the bed. He'd given the light dim command as she crawled onto it. The loose robe caught against the roundness of her buttocks and he'd had to look away as wild heat flooded his veins.

Now, here he lay, and all he wanted was to roll back, away from her siren-like form, but she had burrowed in, her cute little bottom curved in to his groin—the one that currently throbbed with an urgent ache. He swallowed heavily. He'd certainly never experienced this level of arousal with Gospah. So what did that say about him? Galan shied from the question as he shifted himself infinitesimally away. In her sleep Jessa whimpered, burrowed in again and settled herself.

He fought with his conscience. He could wake her. Make love to her. She certainly wouldn't object if her actions earlier were any indicator.

But that would be wrong.

She was under a lot of emotional stresses right now, dealing with her fear from their sudden parting. His breath caught. The pain that had lanced him during her absence was something he didn't want to live through again. The *Quickening* meant that when couples were forced apart they physically yearned for the end of the pain that seared them. But if they chose to part, even for a planned period, he'd heard they weren't bothered by it. A kind of free-will caveat he guessed.

He'd need to ask his father—but not now. He couldn't use the official channels to ask a question such as that. And he certainly wouldn't bring Jessa under that level of scrutiny. With so many now unpartnered, there would be much interest. An interest he feared she would find overwhelming—one that might drive her away.

He still didn't know if he could gain her agreement to go home with him when he retreated from this planet. It meant leaving every-thing she knew behind. He also needed to make a case to the governments here, allowing him to seek several hundred females from this planet for his.

It had been sheer luck that they'd brought the ship to this conti-nent. Seth's contact—the refreshing quality of his welcome the main difference—chosen as the one they'd answered. His crew had triangulated this position and he'd decided it was where they would make landfall.

His side twitched as Jessa shifted restlessly in her sleep. Galan looked down, feeling the warmth steal through his chest. *Smaller.* She was so much tinier than him, but he knew she would fit him perfectly. It made him feel manly and strong. He smiled at his own ruminations as his gaze roamed over her frame. Her perfect and firm breasts looked to be the right size for his hands and his body heated further, leaving him sweating. Her belly slightly rounded, unlike the women he had seen on their broadcasts, stick thin and awkwardly bony. He wanted to touch her skin, feel the weight of her body over his. He groaned slightly. This wasn't helping. But the erotic thoughts continued.

She murmured in her sleep "Galan…" then it became unintelligible once more.

He frowned seeing the shivering of her body as muscles tensed and relaxed. Jessa stiffened again and without thought, Galan wrapped his arms around her. He'd keep the nightmares at bay, he told himself, closing his eyes. Jessa murmured again, this time her shoulder jerked into him. His eyes flashed open.

"Galan… no…" Her words became louder and his stomach clenched.

"Shhh." He whispered into her ear. "It's okay. You're safe now. With me. Galan."

She shuddered and turned into him, now wide awake. "Galan? I had a nightmare." Her chest rose and fell against his arms. It was both agony and ecstasy for him.

"I know. Go back to sleep. I am here."

She hiccupped quietly. "Did I wake you? I'm sorry." She tried to scoot away from him, but he held her in place.

"Stay still. You didn't wake me." He looked into her shining eyes and leaned in, planting a light, soft kiss on her plump pink lips. She moved against him, and he tasted her for just an instant, then pulled back. "Sleep now." The walls glowed with subtle reds and pinks in the dim light. He avoided glancing again, waiting for her to answer him.

She nodded then nestled back, branding him with her touch. He listened for the sound of her breathing to even out once more. But it took a long time for Galan to find his rest.

Chapter 5

Jessa woke to find Galan gone. The bed was still warm though and as she looked at the walls, they shimmered with blues, greens, yellows and even pinks. Obviously she'd passed a peaceful night after her nightmare. Rising quickly, Jessa hurried through her ablutions before she pulled on her clothes. She'd learned during her first visit to drop them into a special cupboard which used ionic waves to clean them. *Whatever that means.* At least she wasn't wearing the same clothes dirty, day after day.

Jessa hurried down the corridor to the meal chamber and was surprised to find Seth sitting by himself. "Hey, you. How are you holding up?"

He gazed at her. "I'm ok. What about you?" Jessa grinned and he patted the comfortably padded seat. "Come and take a load off and talk to me, before the others arrive."

The padded cushions dipped as Jessa slid in beside him. "So, what do you want to talk about?"

"Look, I know I'm not the brightest on the block when it comes to social interactions and all, but honestly... what are you doing with Galan? He's not planning to stay and unless you're intending…" Seth broke off, shock on his face. "You aren't planning on going back with him, are you?"

Something in Jessa's chest started at the proposal. "No! It's not…" She looked around, seeing no one watching. "It's not even been suggested. Besides, he wouldn't want me. You saw his face when I was reminded of my altercation years ago. He's a straight arrow and I've been judged in a court of law. Remember? They convicted me."

Seth leaned in, placing a hand on hers as she looked down, eyes burning. No amount of furious blinking could banish the hot sting of tears as they rolled down her cheeks. She brushed them away with shaking fingers.

"God. I'm sorry Jessa. I didn't mean to…"

She cut him off. "No. You're quite right. I've been living in a fantasy land since this whole thing started. The time has come to realize I can't continue to think everything's going to be fine and dandy. Because it isn't. Do I care for him? Yes, I do." She looked up to Seth's eyes. "But there's no future in thinking that it means he feels the same. The question is where do we go from here?"

Scrubbing the traces of tears from her face was easier than scrubbing him from her heart. But she'd cleared away the traces of tears and stopped hiccupping by the time Galan appeared in the doorway. His face was drawn and tight as he looked for her. Then it seemed to open once more. She wanted to cry again this time at the injustice of life, but there was no benefit in that either. Instead Jessa sucked in deep breaths and hoped no one looked too closely at her.

He sat down and together Seth, Jessa and Galan broke their fast, enjoying some of the delights of Hesparia, including the luscious blue peach and purple nectarine-like fruits. But during the meal her thoughts whirled: Was staying here, on the ship with Galan, the right thing to do?

PARTWAY THROUGH THE MEETING, Jessa excused herself and left the room they'd used over the last several days. She didn't look back, fearing he would read her goodbye in her eyes. Once outside, she met the agent who had stayed with them. "Agent Foley? I have some other tasks to attend to. Can you please make my apologies?" He looked surprised but nodded in silence. Jessa headed the long way, to the back door and exited.

He won't miss me at all. Down the driveway she walked, to the main gate, where lines of angry loud protestors yelled and waved placards. The guards opened the gates for her and she left, gripping her cell phone in one hand as she dialed a taxi.

THE DISCUSSIONS CONTINUED with monotonous rhythm. Galan watched the men in the communication center while his mind tossed and turned realizing that Jessa hadn't returned to the room. *Where has she gone?* After a suitable amount of time had passed, he pushed back his chair and rose. The discussions stopped as all eyes settled on him. But Galan didn't care. Something had happened to Jessa and the urge to find her ballooned. He left the room, his long strides stopped outside the door by human agent who'd accompanied them to the ship the night before. He held up a hand and Galan stopped, cocking his head to one side. "Jessa. Where is she?" The agent grimaced, and a flash of fear coursed through Galan. He controlled it with difficulty. "She's gone, hasn't she?"

The big dark-haired agent opened his mouth and closed it, answering with a single nod. Galan cursed. "When and how?"

"Sir, we believe she slipped through the back of the building. There's an emergency exit there. She was seen leaving the compound. I set an agent to follow her. We know she left in a taxi."

Galan didn't know what a taxi was, but right now that wasn't the issue. Jessa was out there somewhere, far from him. Something he couldn't and wouldn't countenance. Frustration ate at him. *Doesn't she know that she's no ordinary woman now?* A thought occurred to him. With those people outside, what was the chance that she could be in danger? They'd been angry enough the day before to attempt to get to them before they could gain the eli-pad.

His face must have tightened for the agent stepped forward. "She'll be protected for as long as we can manage it." The words didn't dispel the knot of worry that lodged in his chest. Curiously though, the ache in his chest had dissipated. *Did that mean she rejected the Quickening? He knew so little about the physical ramifications...* Perhaps he could enquire of Joras. His friend may know more. But he couldn't right now because of the negotiations and that left him feeling useless.

"Take me to her."

The agent's brows lifted, obviously he hadn't expected that demand, thought Galan mirthlessly. "I'm sorry. I can't do that, Sir." The agent sounded apologetic, but he gave the impression he'd stand firm, no matter what Galan needed.

Galan raised a hand and raked it through his hair as he realized, yet again, that she still didn't have the communicator. It was something he needed to remedy with all speed. Until she at least had that, he wouldn't be able to rest. A beeping sound broke through the air and the agent moved. Galan watched as he spoke into the small device and obviously was angered by the information he was given.

"Yes sir. No sir. We are... Yes sir." The agent winced.

Galan waited, sure the communication was about Jessa.

"Yes sir. Right away." He clicked a button.

For a heartbeat Galan was sure he saw an emotion, which could have been regret pass across the man's face before he shuttered it once more.

"That was my superior. They want us to pull back on detail for Miss Bankia."

Galan bared his teeth in anger. "This is not acceptable."

A careful shrug teamed with, "I'm sorry sir. I can't do anymore."

His mind tumbled and turned as he thought over possibilities. "What if..." He was prepared to take a chance. *Any chance right now.* "What if some of my men needed to explore your habitation? Is that possible?"

"Technically, I doubt my superiors would allow that..." Galan moved in and the agent, Foley held up his hand again. "But, personally your people have shown no aggression towards us. It seems wrong to stop them going about their investigations. Only, your face is already too well known for you to do so. But I'm sure my men will appreciate a little downtime as well."

He let out his breath. At least someone was going to help them —even if it was unofficially.

"But here and now is not the time to discuss it. If you don't mind, sir, I think the negotiating team are looking for you."

Of course. There was sense in his comments. Unable to think clearly, until some sort of resolution had been achieved bothered Galan, however. He was never one to behave this erratically. Surely, he could contain himself to get through this interminable meeting?

BY THE END of the day Galan was strung out. It was decided that he should meet with a delegation from the government of this continent in the morning. It seemed they feared his access to their central city, Canberra. Instead, this Prime Minister and members of her committee would be flown in to this place and meet in a building some distance away from his ship. It would have to be safe from prying eyes, his team argued.

Galan knew that even though this was the first opportunity to enter negotiations, centering on the chance that women would travel to his planet, his concentration was splintered. He'd been made aware that there would be another level of negotiations. Something called the United Nations also had to be involved. The convoluted layers of government alien to his mindset, where there was a simple hierarchy on his own planet. Ruler and Heir were briefed by the Senate who in turn sought the counsel of the local Governors.

Pulling his mind back to his current concerns, he sat down and thought through the steps they had currently taken. Joras had arranged for some of his most trusted security officers to travel with one of the agents beyond the compound. They would go to the most likely place that Jessa would retreat to—her home. Galan wanted to go with them, but Joras had backed up the suggestion that he was already too well known, just as the agent had pointed out.

Instead, he'd stay in his office and work on reports due to go before the Hesparian Senate. *Reports! Bah!* But as captain of the vessel and heir of the royal house, it was his place to set the standard. No matter that he would have preferred to be out there, finding Jessa and bringing her back, he had responsibilities, onerous though they felt right now. The mounting tasks, honor due to his family and his planet rose, along with his frustration at being tied to the desk.

The responsibilities weren't something he was free to flout, instead he dictated to the internal voice driven computer within the ship the details of his current situation, the progress he'd made and the possible alliances that he hoped to forge. He skimmed over Jessa and Seth, for now, choosing to focus on the big picture that would be presented to the senate. Checking and rechecking facts as best he could. Seth was called in to help finalize some details and facts. Then he opened the communication stream to his home world, preparing to send the report to his father.

He concentrated on preparations for the next day, and set about uploading the necessary data to his memory cube, nearly missing the buzzing communicator. He grabbed the device in his hands. "Report."

"Sir, we are at her abode. I believe she lives with her parents, so we need to find a way to make contact without alerting them or the young male of the household." *How many more things can stand in my way?* His shoulders and chest tightened at the possibility that his men could be detected while looking for Jessa. They were among the most loyal of his crew. It could jeopardize the whole mission if they were discovered. The thought weighed heavily on him.

"You have the communicator for her?"

"Yes sir, and details on how to contact the agent with us, if necessary." The arrangements had been made swiftly that evening. It seemed Agent Foley and one of his co-workers had already noted his attachment to her. They'd quickly realized that her loss would be a body blow to Galan. They too had shared his concern given the protestors outside the compound and the lack of interest from their superiors in ensuring the safety of Jessa. Her face and name had apparently been spread by their media outlets meaning she had almost nowhere to hide if things turned ugly. He'd experienced that on other worlds where they'd made first contact and his gut chilled at the thought of what she might face.

"Thank Agent Foley for his understanding." At least one of the agents was focused on a safety network for Jessa. For the next while he paced, unable to settle until he had word that his crew members had made contact with her.

JESSA SAT ON HER BED, feeling sorry for herself. Perhaps Galan had the best of intentions for her, but she couldn't stay. At least that was the pep talk she gave herself. In the back of her mind came the niggle that maybe she'd been wrong and had walked away from the best man—ergo, the best opportunity—to ever come her way. Her eyes ached with unshed tears. It had been very difficult to return home. Jessa's parents had welcomed her by berating her for once more acting without thinking. It always seemed to come back to her one youthful indiscretion.

She'd been eighteen and fancied herself in love with Seth's cousin, Jace but he'd merely used her to gain access to the place where she worked, the local pharmacy. He'd been so attentive. Always taking her to and from work and even walking with her to nightschool, though he had left two years previously. She'd been so sure he was interested in her and *her* only. The laugh over reminiscences sounded bitter, even to her own ears.

One night, she'd been left with instructions to close the shop, given her own key to the front door. Jessa had been over the moon with the responsibility.

Jace had insisted on celebrating, taking her to dinner and she'd stayed the night with him. *The first and only time that happened.* What she hadn't known is that Jace had 'borrowed' her keys and broken in, helping himself to a number of prescription items. Of course, they had worked out it was her key, when they saw the CCTV footage of Jace and she had been arrested as an Accessory. Even now, she felt the indignity of the ink on her fingers as she'd been fingerprinted and when the court date arrived, Jace told his elaborate story. How Jessa had chosen the job, and finally, on gaining their trust, had given him the key so he could access the drugs he sold on her behalf. He'd even brought witnesses to attest to his story.

She'd been lucky to get off with a conviction, suspended sentence and huge fine. Since then, anytime something went wrong, the local police usually called her in, checked her alibi and generally made her life hell. "I'm still paying," she muttered, with the way they'd treated her with the whole first contact thing. Jessa knew she really didn't need any more notoriety. She had experienced enough difficulty getting a job at the observatory.

Her parents were downstairs, resting after fending off the media frenzy that came her way. Weekly and monthly magazines wanted photo shoots, interviews and an insight into her role in the contact situation. The papers, television stations and radio had camped out until she told them bluntly that she knew nothing. The house was starting to finally settle into quietness when something rattled her window. She glanced over to see a hand.

Damn them! I've already told them I know nothing! Jessa stood, anger boiling within her as she marched to the opening, ready to wrench it open and give them a piece of her mind. She stopped short when she got there—a surprising mix of indignation and horror filtering through. It was one of Joras' security detail, his hand extended out to her. She pulled it open and leaned out. "What are you doing?" Her excited whisper stopped him short.

"Galan has sent something for you, but I can't deliver it this way. Is there somewhere we can go?"

His earnest response had her rolling her eyes. *What are they thinking? If they get caught, there'll be hell to pay.* But she nodded. "I'll come down to you." With that she shut the window and turned to the door.

Jessa glanced around the corner. Her parents were engrossed in a current affairs program, so they'd be occupied for a while. As to the location of her brother, well that was anyone's guess. She opened the door and slipped through.

The members of Galan's crew waited in the deep shadows of a weeping willow in the side yard. She glanced around quickly, spotted a man in a suit and dark glasses nearby. If he was trying to look inconspicuous he was failing, she thought with a small hysterical giggle, which she quickly squashed, then gulped. They were about to be caught, but instead he stepped forward with a small smile as her stomach jittered with nerves.

"Miss Bankia, you must be quick. I need to get them back to the compound before they're seen and reported."

How… What..? Jessa shook her head. Now really wasn't the time to be mucking around so she ducked under the hanging greenery to see the two men waiting underneath. "What are you lot doing here?" One she knew slightly for he was a member of Joras' security team.

He bowed low. "Jessa, we bring you a gift from Galan. He is concerned that you will not return in time for the talks that will be held tomorrow."

Oh Lord! Tomorrow? He was going to be meet the PM tomorrow? She gulped swallowing her sense of loss, both at the opportunity to be there when something amazing took place and that she would never see Galan again. She hadn't planned on going back. *Don't they realize that?* "I'm not…returning. I have to resume my normal life, so that once Galan and your crew leaves, I have a job to go back to." She looked at them, earnestly but the other one, the one she didn't know shook his head.

"Galan is lost. He is fretting without your presence. You must return in the morning." He spoke earnestly and the one she knew elbowed him. The speaker gave an audible humph.

Anger flared, white hot within her breast. She didn't *need* to do anything. Jessa made to step away but the one she knew held out a hand. "Jessa, this comes to you from Galan. It's a communicator. He feels that you may be in some danger without the support of the agents looking out for you."

Jessa wanted to scoff, but the memory of the actions of the protestors breaking through containment lines roared into her mind. And the itch at the back of her neck when she left the compound remained with her.

He placed a small item in her hand. It was little bigger than an earring, and she admired it, seeing how beautifully it was engraved. She ran her finger over the edges. "It's exquisite. But how do I...?"

Gently the man showed her the functions, how to contact Galan and how to accept a contact from him. It made no sound until engaged, rather it buzzed like a phone and she smiled. "Isn't it going to look odd having one and not two?" He smiled and retrieved another from his pocket.

"We noticed you wear decorations in your ears. This one is broken, so it will allow you to not stand out too much. Remember, if you get into trouble..."

"Yes, I touch here." Jessa laid her finger on the fine blue stone in the center. "Now, you need to go." A sudden sense of urgency filled her.

Once more, the agent stepped up to her, giving her a piece of paper. "This is my direct cell number. If ever you need help, ring it. I'll do what I can."

Her mouth dried at the thought that she could be in danger. Bravado raised its head; it was probably nothing. But the uneasiness didn't retreat.

From beneath the leaves, she watched as they crept away, carefully shepherded by the agent and got into a small dark car. It pulled away from the curb, leaving her alone. She turned to the house, to feel a hand laid on her shoulder. Jessa jumped, but it was only her brother.

"What did they want?" He watched her intently.

"Nothing. Now don't be so nosey. It's time to go inside." The spot at the back of her neck continued to tingle. Just as she made her way through the door, she glanced around and peered up and down the road. She didn't see anything, so she entered the house and closed the door behind her with a snick.

DAWN CAME and Agent Foley had already rounded Galan up. Not that he'd slept much. His people had arrived back at the ship, smuggled through the gates with some difficulty late at night. His mind had been put at rest, knowing that he at least had some way of contacting Jessa. In his own mind, he had decided to give her time to come to terms with the situation, before he contacted her again— unless she contacted him first. Then, it wouldn't matter what the governing body had to say, he'd send his men to retrieve her because she appeared innocent in all the machinations. Those of the past and the current situation.

Galan ate and drank, and it felt little more than a chore then he stood, checking for the small memory cube he was taking with him. He and Joras donned their ceremonial robes agreeing to make their entrance using the light based camouflage. It usually put others on the back foot and given he was the only member of his house present, he'd take any advantage. Dealing with the female they called their Prime Minister had put in his mind, the need to ensure he had taken every chance to strengthen their case. His dealings so far, had told him she was more slippery than a ground slither and frustratingly obnoxious too. He'd have to watch his step as much as his temper.

Together they made their way down the corridor to the eli-pad to meet the increased security detail assembled for the excursion to the burg of Parkes. A processions of large vehicles had been placed at their disposal for transport to and from the venue and Galan looked at it, noting the rudimentary nature of the vehicles. He'd have preferred to use one of their own conveyances, but Agent Foley stated that this would probably cause more issues than it would solve.

He clambered in, grunting as he moved into the restrictive space. "Please use the seatbelt."

Galan looked at the driver. *What's a seatbelt?* Galan looked at Foley.

"I have no idea what a seat belt is. Can you please explain this?"

Seth climbed in beside him. "Joras thought you might need some assistance." Seth grinned at Galan before he rolled his eyes.

"I need to use a seat belt." He carefully enunciated each word and was startled when Seth leaned over him. "What are you doing, Seth?"

"I'm putting your seatbelt on. So, watch and learn. That way you can do it by yourself on the way back." A thin strap of webbing was drawn over his shoulder and clicked into a small metal clasp. Galan was fascinated. On Hesparia they used force fields on their small conveyances, so it was rare that anyone got more than a bump or bruise.

A whine rent the air and he sat up, startled. *Surely they aren't still using internal combustion engines for formal occasions?* Galan made a note to ask about that later as they pulled out. He watched as they drove along, small single conveyances moved ahead with flashing lights attached to the front, and the person rode astride another smaller machines they named motorbike. Galan watched as other vehicles stopped for them as they headed into the township.

It wasn't so very small as he was led to believe, more the size of one of the agricultural townships that provided produce to Hesparian cities. Greenery lined the roads they travelled on and small mercantiles were dotted here and there. The houses were mainly neat and tidy. Occasionally some people along the roadside waved signs at the vehicles as they drove through the streets until they reached a large white building. It was ugly and stark white, resembling a glorified box sitting in the center of town with perfectly aligned garden beds.

"Well, this is it." Seth looked at him nervously. "Do you think you can undo the seatbelt? There is a small button to release it."

Galan nodded and found the clip, releasing the belt with a hiss. Seth climbed out and Galan followed him, smoothing down his ceremonial garb. He stepped away from the vehicle and while Seth closed the car door he remembered to turn on the light camouflage.

Audible gasps broke out as Galan watched the vehicle roll away. He was ushered within the interior of the building. With a shrug Galan entered the structure, feeling the caress of the cool air.

Sounds from outside were muted once he'd retreated inside and the door closed. Galan scanned his surroundings, looking at the glass boxed items with an interested eye. A buzz at his collar caught his attention. "Galan."

"Well, gee thanks Galan. I called to you and they won't let me through." Jessa. *"Is there something I need to know? Some reason I'm not being included?"*

"Wait one moment, while I request you be escorted inside." He grinned, uncaring who noted it and didn't attempt to hide the jaunty spring in his step. Ever since his men had returned from Jessa's abode, he'd been concerned that she wouldn't attend the meeting. But no, here she was. A warm tide of elation swept through him. He turned to Agent Foley. "Jessa is just beyond the door. Please have her escorted in."

Agent Foley looked at him and something shifted within him. "I'm sorry, Sir. I can't."

Galan stilled and looked at the man. "Can't or won't?"

"Can't, Sir. My orders are that Miss Bankia is to be refused entrance." The words were as impassive as his facial expression.

"Galan? What the hell is going on? They say I am on the Do Not Allow list. "

"Jessa, I am currently discussing the situation inside. Stay where you are." His words were precise, and he was sure he heard a comment.

"Do you think you could hurry it up a little?"

Frustration was clear in her voice and he wanted to smile yet smothered the grin. "No Jessa, no co-operation." Galan hardened his voice speaking to Agent Foley.

Agent Foley nodded and turned away, talking into his phone and Galan waited.

"Sir, I can't…"

"Fine. Joras? We leave now." The security detail formed a circle around him and they headed for the door. Shouts broke out behind him, but he didn't turn, until one strident female voice called out.

"Let her in!"

Galan stopped and waited. Were they planning to let Jessa join them, now? Was this how it was going to be played out? Brinkmanship all the way? His gut churned while fury rose, but he contained it. The glass door opened and Jessa scurried in. He let himself gaze upon her, the vibrant green of her skirt and the white shirt emphasized her loveliness. Her face pinked and the glitter in her eyes called to him. She was his. He would never give her up. Not now. Not ever.

She wore the communicator and the non-functional unit as ear adornments. Her red hair tied back, showing the long line of her throat and her legs were bare. On her feet were green shoes which matched her skirt while over her shoulder was slung a small bag. Without a doubt she was both the most feminine and the most beautiful female in the room. All the other women wore tailored pants and what appeared to be mens shirts, negating any femininity that they projected. She joined the group of Hesparians, a small smile playing over her features and his breathing eased.

JESSA HADN'T MEANT to join them. In fact, she'd been determined to go back to her nice safe and totally neutral lifestyle, which included work and home. Nothing more than resuming her life had been in her conscious mind. She'd dressed for work at the observatory in her customary skirt and blouse, but subconsciously, she followed the buzz of excitement to the community center. Her feet finding their way here as if some primal force told her she needed to be by his side. So she'd obeyed and even wore his earrings, not that she knew why and that made her feel like a prize fool.

Anger filled her remembering the confrontation outside. The person on the door had flushed once she had gained entrance. Refused indeed! Thank heavens she'd had the communicator which meant she could tell Galan she was outside. She didn't know what he'd said, but made a point to ask him later. Her fingers itched to fiddle with her skirt ensuring it sat correctly. It was just nerves of course, but she couldn't help her reaction in front of these important people. She wanted to show herself in the best possible light before him, which was silly, but it didn't stop the ingrained feminine pleasure she derived from watching him look her over.

Slow steps brought her to him. He smiled slightly, and she melted deep inside. Seth grinned and elbowed her in the ribs, the quick sting calling her back from the introspective fog she had lost herself in on seeing Galan. Jessa realized what a spectacle she was making of herself and him too. "So… Are you ready Galan?"

He nodded in silence. She joined the group heading towards the door.

Jessa scanned the room, she'd been here many times, attending functions with her parents and brother, but it had never looked like this before. People milled here and there in small groups, phones stuck to ears. They talked in earnest but muted whispers as others tapped on their tablet devices, no doubt sending requests to their minions back in offices in Canberra. As they passed, she saw others looking at them. She shivered, feeling so out of place among these career politicians and public servants. Galan's hand rested lightly on Jessa's waist, making her nerve endings quiver in reaction to his careless caress.

"Look, it's the PM." Seth's scornful voice caught her attention.

She glanced in the direction he indicated. The Prime Minister was taking her seat, talking quietly before holding up a hand, cutting her staffers off. The men and women's expressions showed acceptance of her curt action and the Prime Minister smiled at Galan. A well-practiced curve of her lips. One she had obviously used thousands of times before, but Jessa was unsurprised to see it didn't reach her eyes. No, those contained a calculating directness. She stood and walked slowly in the direction of their group.

"Welcome Captain Galan." She stuck her hand out to him.

Jessa was impressed by how effectively she cut off the rest of the group with the single motion.

"I'm so pleased you chose Australia as your first landing site." The woman didn't gush or fawn over him, but worked steadily, drawing Galan away from the group. Seth and Jessa waited, and for her part, she was unsure what to do or how to react. *Should we follow? Should we wait?*

Joras moved beside Jessa. "Do you know this woman?"

"She's the Prime Minister. The head of our elected government." Jessa answered absently while her eyes took in every carefully rehearsed step.

"Hmm. Is this the norm for the way she meets with dignitaries, find one and single them out from the others? It isn't very…wise, surely?" His dry words made Jessa want to smile.

"I don't know. I've never met her before." She stepped forward but Joras touched her arm slightly.

"Let's wait and see what happens, shall we?" His voice held amusement. She turned to see a glint of humor in his eyes.

They waited and soon enough Galan bowed in a courtly manner and returned to their group, indicating each member and making an introduction as he went. Once this happened, they were ushered to seats at the long white clad table.

"Jessa and Seth will be seated with my crew," insisted Galan and the meeting came to order. The members of the working group ran through the usual processes and Jessa sat, pen in hand and scribbled notes on the small pad placed before her.

Quickly, it came time for Galan to outline the issue. "We have come to earth seeking assistance. We have, in the last several years, lost many of the females from our planet. We come seeking willing volunteers to join us on Hesparia." As he spoke the room erupted in murmurs and she could see heads shaking.

"Madam Prime Minister…" A large man in a suit rose to his feet, his face thunderous. "You cannot possibly allow…"

The Prime Minister stood, raising a hand. "Please resume your seat, Minister. We shall discuss this later." He looked at her, red faced before slowly subsiding into his chair. She returned steely eyes back to Galan. "Please, continue Captain."

Jessa contained her snort of amusement. It was clear Galan hadn't informed the PM of his real status or position. "Thank you, Prime Minister. In exchange, we are more than happy to share insights into genetic technology, space flight and healing with your people."

The shocked murmurs continued as the discussion turned to timeframes, goodwill gestures. A meal was delivered to the table, yet the humans kept a watchful eye on their Hesparian counterparts. Jessa sighed each time another objected to something Galan mentioned or offered.

By the end of the meeting, she was exhausted and wanted nothing more than to sit down with a quiet drink. *Preferably something long and cold and decidedly alcoholic*, she told herself. Agent Foley made his way over to her, she hadn't heard him approach but quickly turned in his direction at his words. "Miss Bankia?"

"Yes, Agent Foley?"

He looked slightly discomforted. "Can you please tell me if it is your intention to stay with the Hesparians? We seem to be having some trouble working out exactly where you're supposed to be billeted."

As Jessa made to open her mouth, Galan moved behind her, slipping an arm around her shoulder as he addressed the agent. "Jessa will remain with me, so if you could make arrangements for suitable clothing and effects to be delivered to my ship? I will require the same, of course, for Seth."

As quickly as that, the matter was settled.

Then they were moved through the door, and to the cars that waited in the portico.

Voices called and lights flashed but Galan kept her at his side. Jessa scanned the crowd and at the back she saw a face. One she hadn't seen for a long time. One she had thought she'd wake up next to, for the rest of her adult life when she was much younger and so much more naïve. *Jace.*

Chapter 6

Days passed, each full of meetings. Jessa remained with Galan, Seth and the crew on what she learned was the *Princess Gospah*. They took delegations and even made a trip to Canberra, flanked by military personnel. As the days had progressed the protestors became more strident and increased in numbers. Each time she saw their hatred and heard their angry words, Jessa shivered. She scanned the crowds, sure that Jace was there. But what on earth could he want? Certainly not her, the thought had spun around in her head day and night.

She did learn more about how the Hesparian's had such a grasp of their language though as they broke their fast one morning.

A thought occurred to Jessa. "Hang on. Something has just occurred to me. Even after our first meetings you have an extraordinary grasp of our language."

Joras grinned. "We had been monitoring your planet for some time, and found that we could decode your language very quickly through your written and spoken translations. And of course, we availed ourselves of some of your transmissions. I believe you call it tele-vis-eon."

Of course they would. She rolled her eyes, noting the careful way he pronounced the words They must have learnt some very interesting things from the current crop of shows.

Soldiers were brought in to guard the perimeter and Jessa watched in amazement as her countrymen spewed vitriol in the media. Their angry comments about letting aliens walk on their planet and possibly even mate with them worried her. Others claimed that those who'd associated with them were now somehow tainted. Radio talk shows were flooded with arguments that: *No human should be expected to participate in what was essentially a bride buyout for another planet! The end of the world is here!* And, *is this the beginning of the alien invasion?*

Her mother and father both contacted her via cell. Her mother castigating her for being involved and once they knew what the Hesparians were doing. "You're participating in something that's little more than slavery of a galactic nature." Their cold comments stung and Jessa started screening calls, ignoring their messages. Emails poured in to her from radio and television stations once more, flooding her spam folder and deleted box.

ON A MORNING little over a week after their initial meeting with the Prime Minister, Jessa sat in the dining room looking at the emails flooding in, her laptop whizzing happily. "You know Jessa, the only thing you have to worry about right now, is whether you stay or go." Seth's words had her jumping as he entered the quiet room.

"Oh, that's so easy for you to say, Seth. You know he hasn't even asked me. Besides which, even if the United Nations decides to go along with this crazy idea, they'll want to vet everyone involved. I doubt I'd even get a look in."

He snorted, and Jessa raised her head. "Are you laughing at me?"

He sobered, sitting down beside her. "No, but I'm trying to

lighten your mood a little. I doubt either of us will be welcome here once this is done."

She looked at him, noting the circles under his eyes and the way he ran his hand through his shaggy red hair. "Are you okay?" Concern flooded her. In her own misery and confusion, she really hadn't been paying attention to him. Looking now, it was clear how strained he'd become.

"Yeah, I'm fine." But clearly he wasn't.

"Come on Seth. This is me you're talking to. Remember?" She laid her hand on his. "You can tell me."

"Well, to be honest, it's true. You at least will be able to leave, but me? They won't have use for another male. And one who isn't married or in a relationship?" He shrugged, looking dejected and lost. Jessa's heart plummeted to her stomach with a dipping sensation. "And I doubt there's going to be anywhere here that would either hire me or for that matter, want me within a twenty-mile radius if any of the comments on the news are anything to go by."

Holy hell. That hadn't even occurred to her. "Oh, Seth. Maybe…" But he cut her off.

"What? You'll talk to Galan. If you don't think he'll take you, can you honestly see him accepting me?"

They were in a fine pickle, Jessa thought. Feeling even more down than before because these were truths that they both had to face, a sense of loss swamped her for a moment. Then with a small sigh she sat upright once more. "Geez. I hadn't even thought about that." She slumped down to the table top just as the ding of new mail filled the air.

"You'd better check that." Seth mumbled laying his head down on the table.

Jessa opened the new mail and shock stole her breath.

"What is it?" Seth raised his head and looked into her eyes.

"It's from Jace. I don't know how he even got my email address." Shock tightened her lips and her heart pounded. "I don't want to hear from him, Seth. I mean…"

"Who has contacted you?" Galan demanded from the doorway.

Jessa closed her eyes. *Great. That's all I need. To remind him of my checkered past.*

"It's my cousin. Jace" Seth's voice rang out and Jessa would have given anything right now for a hole in the ground—somewhere to hide in.

"And this is a problem, Jessa?" He moved forward placing a hand on her shoulder.

Jessa fought the urge to curl into his touch. This was her problem. One she had to stand alone and deal with. "He's the one I did something stupid with. The one that…" A lump lodged in her throat.

"He told a lie about Jessa and got her in a lot of trouble." Seth's voice broke the pregnant silence. "Jessa was innocent in the whole thing."

"Hush, Seth." Jessa turned to look at him. "I was young. I was dumb and I let him use me. I had to pay some penalty for that." She shrugged. "But it'll never happen again."

Galan lifted his hand from her shoulder and that one action gutted her to the soul.

GALAN'S ANGER BURNED BRIGHTLY. White hot rage coursed through his veins as his belly churned. That this *Jace* had dared to contact Jessa was indeed a problem he needed to address. Then there was the manner in which the rest of the government of earth were acting. It was enough to make him want to give up on the whole idea of seeking women from this planet. Surely his people could find other compatible planets? But even as the thought came, he dismissed it with a flick of his eyes. He glanced down at Jessa, caught sight of her white face. "What? What more are you not telling me?" His heart stuttered, and he reached for her.

"It's nothing." Her voice was low and pain filled.

Seth rose, catching his eye. "We all need to talk later. But right now, I'll leave you two alone." He left the room quickly.

Galan glanced back to her, seeing her downcast eyes. "Jessa?" He wanted to understand. He needed to know what the problem was so he could help her...make it better for her.

"It's nothing Galan."

"That's not true. Otherwise you wouldn't be shaking like a leaf. Now, tell me what the problem is."

"You can't fix this." Her voice was thready and his stomach knotted tighter than before in reaction.

"I can."

"No, actually. This time you can't. When this is done..." She stopped, and he craned further.

"When this is done, what?"

"It's nothing." She started poking and prodding at the small terminal in front of her.

"You can't say that and then not finish what you mean. Jessa..." *How can I reach her, when she won't tell me what's wrong?*

Jessa stood up jerkily and he grabbed her hand. The computer slipped and dropped to the floor, smashing loudly.

"When this is over, you'll be gone and Seth and I will be here. We'll have to make the best of this...mess!" She cried.

Finally, he understood. The memory of the negative emotion, of loss, flooded him. He refused to let her feel it any longer. "I won't leave you behind. Or Seth, for that matter." He gazed at her, taking in the soul-deep sadness in her eyes. The emotion scalded him, leaving him almost breathless at the pain that ratcheted through his system.

She snorted at his words. "Like you'll have any other option."

He grabbed her to him and snarled, "I won't! I won't ever let you go. You're mine now!" And with that he swooped down, catching her lips with his. The kiss was brutal as his mouth roamed over hers. He molded her tight against his frame, learned the dips and swells of her body. His mind whirled at the taste and feel of her. Finally, gasping for breath he pulled away. "I'm not letting you go." He gripped her hand and towed her out of the room and down the corridor.

The door of her cabin opened, and he pulled her into the quiet room, bringing her back up against his body. "Does this feel like a man who will leave you behind?"

She stared at him, shock clear on her face. "But...Galan..." Then she blushed, the red tide rising on her pale skin.

His mind whirled as a primal thrill rushed through his body.

"Yes." The single word echoed through the silence.

"You will stay with me, then?"

"Yes." She gulped.

"Be sure. *I will not ever* let you leave me." He bit the words out then he dipped down, until his mouth was level with hers and she gave a sigh. He felt her reach up, catch her fingers behind his head and she opened her mouth to his tongue.

He was lost in the maelstrom of passion.

Galan cupped her breast, while he touched and mapped her body, hyper aware of her nipples as they budded against his chest. He pulled away. "You're mine. You know it, don't you?"

She shivered in his arms and he waited for her to acknowledge his words.

"I'm...Galan, I..."

"Mine." He growled the single word as primal triumph roared through him.

THE FEELINGS he evoked in her were wild. She wanted him. Every fiber of her body cried out for his touch. His caress. Jessa quivered in his arms, glorying in the sensations he invoked. The feel of him pushed up tight against her left her gasping for breath. He was so big! It made her feel cherished and safe... *and wanted.*

Against her own will, Jessa moaned slightly, needing more of the drug-like kisses that filled her up.

He laughed lightly. "Soon, my beautiful. We will not rush this though."

"Galan, I want..."

He stilled as if waiting for her refusal and she swallowed past the lump that had lodged in her throat, seeking a boldness she had never before possessed. She gulped, as she finally understood that he felt as uncertain as she did. "I want... you." The words rushed out and he smiled, her knees turned to water at the gleam in his eyes.

He moved quickly, crushing his mouth to hers and he thrust his tongue within the welcoming cavern.

They tangled and she gloried in the sense of rightness. His sure hands roamed over her body, igniting small wildfires everywhere he touched. A slip here, just across her buttocks and a caress there at her shoulder, left her aching with the promise of pleasure yet to come.

Oh God! She was so turned-on by this man. She didn't know how he did it, but she wanted more!

Jessa tangled her fingers in his hair then moving to his shoulders, learning the shape of him, before dropping to his chest. Savoring the feel of corded muscles below the cotton which kept her from the skin she so desperately needed to touch.

He found the fasteners of her blouse, deftly twisting a button through the hole before he burrowed in beneath the thin material. His light and questing touch on her stomach had her tugged away with a gasp.

"How do I...?" He pulled away and she saw his passion glazed eyes then he hurried on to his own suit fastenings, shaking with the intensity of their passion. Then the top half was gone, baring his skin to her wandering gaze. Muscles rippled as she stared. *It's all mine for the taking.*

Her mouth dried and she chanced a look at his face. "You like what you see, don't you Jessa?" His voice was hypnotic and she nodded slowly before she lifted trembling hands to the fasteners he hadn't yet toyed with, slipping them through the holes. She watched him, his hooded gaze smoky and intense. And she rejoiced in the feminine power she had over this man.

Jessa pulled the blouse from her body, extended her hand and let the item fall to the floor. Then it was forgotten as the sound of his heavy breathing filled the silence. She waited for his response, her stomach twisting and churning wildly.

Galan's gaze dipped to her breasts, hidden only by a plain cotton bra. They weren't large and she had many times wished they were more enticing. Now she wanted him to see them, touch them and find them just right, even if they were only covered by dowdy underwear. She silently cursed that she owned no sexy lingerie for this man to see her in.

"You are truly the most beautiful woman I have ever seen." She shivered at his words as he extended his hands to cup her twin globes. He grazed the sensitive nubs through her bra and she whimpered.

Slowly he moved his fingers to the straps, toying with them as he grazed over them—up and down over the light cups, each pass running ever so slightly over her nipples. Jessa wanted to cry out at the pleasure his touch evoked.

"I'm going to love you. I'm going to touch you and I'm going to pleasure you. Because you are mine."

Her eyes closed at his words.

Klaxons wailed and the lights flickered on and off. Galan pulled away. "Stay here." He jack-knifed up quickly, collecting his shirt and shrugging it on. "It will be safer." Then he was gone, leaving her alone in the room.

Jessa headed slowly to the bed. Her chest heavy and her breathing hadn't slowed much. Her body remained fired up and she squeezed her legs together vainly hoping to settle the arousal spiking through her. The wail of the klaxon ended as miserable tears rolled down her face.

So close!

She sighed, wiping a hand across her face… Jessa struggled to contain herself. "God knows it nearly happened and the damn alarms go off." As the importance of that filtered back into her consciousness, she grimaced. "I hope it wasn't anything too bad." she muttered aloud and jumped at the voice that sounded through the room.

"No Jessa. It was an incursion that was quickly dealt with. I believe Galan has given orders and is returning to you right now." The walls glowed shades of blue, green and yellow as the perfectly modulated voice startled her.

"Who said that?" Fear snaked through her.

The chime of laughter filled the air. "It is me. The Princess Gospah."

The what? Holy hell, the ship can talk?

"No. No ship can talk." She waited, curling the fingers of one hand against her chest, while she hauled on the bedding to cover herself.

"Alas, Jessa, I can. I know Galan has not explained about me yet. I am a sentient species and offer my services to those of pacifist leanings. I and my brethren have been with the Hesparians for generations."

Jessa gasped at the explanation. *Sentient ships?* For a moment, she wanted to laugh and believe it was a hoax. But the next thought stopped it in its tracks. *Hadn't that also been the common theory about long distance space travel? That it was a fantasy which humans wouldn't achieve in a single lifetime?* At least until the Hesparians had come on the scene.

"I will leave you now. But please be at peace knowing we respect the privacy of those who travel aboard us." The room colour changed to a light blush pink and Jessa was sure it meant she was alone once more.

The door slid open and in walked Galan. "Jessa, forgive me." He reached out a hand in entreaty.

"Why didn't you tell me?" She blurted out her demand and he stopped dead.

"Tell you what?" He looked puzzled.

"About the ship. That it can *talk* and is sentient."

He looked at her and smiled. "Would you have believed it beforehand?" He stepped closer. "I know the interruption was ill timed, but do you think…?"

She stared at him. "What? You want me to…?" She waved a hand in the air and his smile deepened. "After that? How can I be sure…*she* …*it*…?' *Arrgh!*" Jessa shook her head from side to side. "How do we know that no one is listening?"

"The wall colors." He looked at her.

She squinted. "Sorry?"

"The wall colors mute when she is not here. She can choose whether or not to be within the room. Right now, she isn't. It's a muted colour. If the colors are bright you can usually tell. But the *Princess Gospah* will also withdraw when couples wish to be…intimate."

"I don't know…" She whispered the words, wanting to be with him in every way and worried that the ship would be a voyeur.

"Jessa…" Galan leaned in and kissed her softly. "*Trust me.*"

But she couldn't let go yet. Jessa stood and moved away. "What happened?" She changed the subject and Galan sighed heavily. Jessa knew it wasn't totally fair to him, but she needed to know why. What had caused the alarm before she could give herself over to him.

"A man made for the ship and tried to get in." He harrumphed and sat himself down on the end of the bed. "At least come and sit down beside me if you want to talk."

She eyed him cautiously then nodded, before making her way over to him. "And?"

"He tried to break one of the plates that protects Gospah in space. Fortunately our own security men were on hand and dealt with the situation quickly. I only saw as he was taken away."

"So, the threat is over?"

"Yes, Jessa. He has been dealt with and I hope we won't see any more of him." Galan shook his head. "Now, I believe that maybe I should leave you alone." His words sent a spurt of pain through her system.

She didn't know if she was ready for the intimacy, but even more so, she didn't want him to leave. He stood and she reached out a hand. "No. Please…don't go…"

"Jessa, I can't…"

"I know. I needed to be sure." Jessa sucked in a deep lungful of air, then she whispered, "And I am."

Once she had made her decision, she knew it was right. She

reached one hand behind her back and he sat on the bed watching. *Oh man. I've never done this before.* Her fingers shook on the clasp and she fumbled a little before feeling the give in her bra. Finally it gaped away from her body and she shivered a little, wondering what he would say.

A soft sound emanated from Galan and he smiled, just a small uptick at the corner of his mouth, but enough to let her know he liked what he was seeing.

"Your turn." She whispered the words, emboldened.

He stood, reaching for his shirt before he stripped it away. Her heart thumped madly.

"Uh uh. More. I saw that last time. Show me something new."

His smile broadened and he reached for his pants. Her breath caught as he inched them down, a flash of white caught her eye and he smirked. They dropped to the floor with a thud and he stepped out of them. He was left wearing what looked like over long boxers, tied with a cord. She moaned noting how they sat on his hips, dipping ever so slightly to his groin.

"Not fair." She breathed the words and he chuckled. She watched mesmerized as his chest moved with the sound. She needed to touch his flesh. She stepped forward so that she now stood within touching distance of him. Extended one finger and made contact before pulling it away.

Electric. Sparks of arousal flew through her body and she gasped in reaction.

"I want to touch you." His guttural words filled her body with heat and she nodded wordlessly.

He reached out to her, a finger first caressed her shoulder before lightly sliding down her arm. "So beautiful. And all mine."

She shuddered at his words as she caressed him, feeling the dips and hollows of his chest and up to his collarbone. So firm and warm and she wanted more—needed more.

Her secret recesses heated and grew damp while he touched the tip of her breast. Her knees buckled and he grabbed her up, lifting her to the bed even as he fastened his mouth over hers. Jessa let her tongue touch his while he roamed his hands over her body, searching for the hem of the skirt she wore and shoving it out of the way. Galan's hard fingers kneaded her thighs until they opened.

Jessa tugged on the tie at his waist. Mindless need filled her and she arched as he moved his lips down her neck, finding the most sensitive spot on her collarbone, using his tongue to lave her skin.

"Oh God!" She bucked as he found her panties and burrowed below, seeking the entrance to her core.

"Naked. We need to be naked." She panted the words and pushed at him.

He levered himself away shucking his under things while she made short work of her skirt and panties. Then they were naked and skin to skin. She got a glimpse before he covered her once more with his body. His erection magnificent and at the tip a bead of moisture seeped slightly.

Galan caressed the downy hair at her apex as they kissed. Strong fingers grazed the sensitive skin of her cleft, making her squirm with excitement. She arched into him, knowing that her release was close. He slipped a finger within and she nearly came with the exquisite feeling. She groped for and found him, fondling the tip, now engorged and pulsing.

"Inside me Galan. I need you now!"

He jack-knifed up. Fitting himself against her and in one quick thrust pushed himself to the hilt inside her.

Then they moved, both rocking against the other as she gripped his shoulders. "More."

"Yes," he cried hoarsely, his lips once again against her neck. She tensed against him. Her body spasming rhythmically around him and he moved one more time.

She felt the jetting of his release deep within her and exulted in it. Never before had the sensations been like this. Sex, well the couple of times she had tried it, had been marginally warm. Never hot and frenzied like this.

He rolled, pulling her with him. "Now you are truly mine. In every way that counts." Jessa noticed the deep reds on the walls and cringed. She'd totally forgotten that the ship was sentient.

"Oh God." She groaned the words and Galan looked at her.

"What?" His eyes narrowed. "You aren't going to regret this now, are you?"

Jessa shook her head. "No. But the...*this ship*? Did it hear us?" She glanced nervously around.

He laughed and the rumble of his muscles against her still highly sensitized body left her tingling once more in sensual reaction. "No, she withdrew."

Jessa looked around. "But the room. It's glowing with red... I mean, what does that mean?"

He must have heard the bewilderment in her tone and he chuckled once again. "The room reacts to our emotions. This is the after passion red. If you had been paying attention beforehand, it would have been even brighter than this."

She looked at him. *Really? Amazing. Who would have ever thought of this, even in their wildest dreams?* Jessa couldn't contain the blush that suffused her body, but she cuddled up against Galan. Her life had certainly changed since the phone call from Seth that fateful evening. What was it? Less than a fortnight ago? But she still wasn't sure what the future held for her. "Galan?" She levered up onto one elbow.

"Hmm?"

"What's going to happen to Seth and I? I mean, knowing the government...they aren't going to let just anyone go to Hesparia. And with my background, I sincerely doubt I would even get a look in."

"I don't see that it should be their choice. Both you and Seth are members of the crew now. We won't leave you behind." He said the words, but the seed of doubt remained.

"So just how do you plan to move that many women on this one ship, anyway?" It wasn't a huge ship and from what she could see, it was nowhere near large enough to move that many extra people.

He smiled, running his hand over her hair. "You really want to discuss this now?"

She tapped his abdomen. "Yep." She grinned at his pained expression.

"Okay then. We have another ship, behind the moon. Just

waiting for the go ahead and we will act as a transport to and from the ship. It's too large to make landing, but has adequate berth facilities." He sighed. "Now, are you satisfied?" He looked so put upon that she laughed.

"Not quite." With those words she dipped her head forward for a heated kiss.

Chapter 7

This time when Jessa emerged from her room, she felt loose and energized. Ready to meet any challenge life threw at her. They moved together down the corridor. Not quite hand in hand, but close enough to be able to touch. She smiled to herself, Galan was a caring lover and she knew the stars had been in alignment on the day they met.

They entered an office she hadn't been in before. Joras and Seth sat at a table, deep in conversation. Seth looked up, took a second harder look and nodded as if he knew what they had been doing. Jessa blushed a deep, almost beetroot red she was sure, as her face flamed. Not that she was embarrassed…much. Still, Seth knowing she had slept with Galan after their conversation was a touch…well, *embarrassing.*

"Galan, we have been requested to meet with their United Nations. I have accepted on your behalf." Joras' voice showed no knowledge of their intimacy, but one thing she had learned during their time on the *Princess Gospah* was that Joras rarely showed what he was thinking or feeling, playing everything very close to his chest. Jessa thought perhaps it was something he only showed with those closest to him.

He indicated to chairs for the two of them and they sat, while Joras handed a tablet device to Galan. The runes and shapes still meant little to Jessa, but determination filled her. *She would learn to read and write in their language too, even if he did leave her behind.*

They discussed how they would travel to the United Nations.

"The humans have indicated they wish you to use their transport."

Jessa watched as Galan grunted. "Our own would give us freedom."

"Perhaps, Galan. But this is a show of goodwill and one we need badly if we're to gain their trust and assistance."

Galan frowned, then gave a nod. "Very well then. Make the arrangements." Resolved that they would travel the next day to meet the Prime Minister at the military aerodrome located in Richmond, using their government sanctioned vehicles, Jessa's stomach wobbled while it was clear Galan was less than impressed that they would take upwards of a week between meetings and travel. Seth shrugged his shoulders, explaining that their planes didn't have the capabilities of Hesparia's, from what he understood.

"Perhaps, Seth, but our conveyance would be faster and infinitely more comfortable. Joras, ensure Seth and Jessa travel with us. As our liaisons."

They put together a list of resources, images and information they thought might help to sway the situation and Jessa watched as they both worked with efficiency. Seth worked at something that looked remarkably like a primer and Jessa wondered what skills she had to offer in the negotiations before she sighed heavily.

"What worries you?" Galan's voice dipped low and a warm tide spread through her belly.

"I just don't feel I have anything to offer. You know? In the negotiations."

"Of course you do." Galan kept working even as he said the words, but they seemed absent to her. Almost as if they were an automatic response.

"I don't."

"Jessa, you're much better than me at spelling and writing, plus you did all the initial translations. How about we work together on this Hesparian and English language dictionary?" Seth's voice called across the room and Galan quirked his brow. She let out a frustrated huff and wandered over to stand behind Seth. She watched as he struggled to input the information into his laptop while balancing the tablet.

"I can do that." She sat herself down and was quickly immersed in the task, typing in the words, finding a phonetic spelling that allowed her to adequately create an English version.

"Jessa?"

She raised her head. "What?"

She looked at Galan who was smiling down at her.

"It is time to eat. Come. We will join the crew in the meal area."

"But we've only just started." She grimaced, but Galan just grinned at her.

"You have been working for hoors."

Jessa giggled, pleased at his attempt to use her language. "You mean hours." But she rose anyway accepting the hand he held out for her. Seth sent a highly amused glance her way and she snickered before he and Joras joined them.

They found the rest of the crew in a festive mood. The meal was perfectly delicious, though she had no idea what it was. The lightly spiced meat was succulent, Galan had assured her it was low in fat and high in protein. He'd mentioned the animal it came from but it was meaningless to her. The tubers were tender and tasted divine, even if they were blue. She insisted that they order some local delicacies be brought aboard, including lamingtons and pavlovas, bananas and coconuts, even lychees and the delicious tropical star fruit. She could see the crewmembers eagerly devouring them.

"Do you usually eat like this?" She extended her hand.

"What, as a group?"

Jessa laughed. "No, I meant with such foods? And options?"

He looked at her and smiled. "Our planet is mainly agrarian, so we grow our own meats and vegetables. Everyone is encouraged to participate in the welfare of our planet and we take a dim view on those who don't. Of course, there are some members who cannot help, such as the aged and infirm. In those cases, their foods are provided and highly nutritious. Our healers ensure that they are comfortable and well-nourished at all times. They've already done their service for the planet and we thank them in kind." He stopped and looked at her. "But that isn't what you want to know. Yes, we do eat well at our meals. Many participate in communal repasts, ensuring that there is a variety in their diets that they might not enjoy if they prepared foods for just themselves."

Jessa thought over his words. It seemed almost utopian, but there had to be a fly in the ointment apart from the loss of the child bearing women. "What about crime? Is that a problem?"

"We have those who do not wish to adhere to our rules. We try to educate and help those who wish to make a change, but at the end of the day, some will not and do not wish to live the way we do. We give them options to leave the planet or to remove themselves to the far continent. Usually they choose to leave and in those situations we offer them assistance to travel and start a new life." Galan looked down at the table. "From time to time, we must use punitive measures, but that is not a lightly taken decision. In the end, those measures are enacted with a view to the betterment of our society and may include undertaking labor for those who cannot provide their own under instruction."

She watched the play of his face, sensing that he truly believed his words. Could it be true? Could the Hesparian society be so calm and pacific? She needed to know more. "And the children?"

He blanched and she remembered the state of affairs. "Oh, I'm sorry Galan."

He shook his head with an odd smile. "The odd child may be recalcitrant too. In those instances, we attempt to correct their behavior in a loving manner."

Jessa sighed. Even on the utopian planet of Hesparia there was the criminal element.

By the end of the meal Jessa had decided that no matter if it wasn't rosy, it had to be better than her situation here, on earth, and the dismal future that loomed.

GALAN WOKE SLOWLY, the unfamiliar weight at his side momentarily surprising him before he smiled. *Jessa.* Finally she was where she belonged—in his arms. Last night they had both fallen exhausted into the bed, but in the night she'd spooned up against him in a most delightful manner. Her pert bottom nestled against him and her head rested on the pillow, her skin pale against the green of the linens. Careful, so as not to wake her, he stroked her silky red hair. Delight filled him as he considered their conversation from the night before as they broke their fast. Her questions showed a keen interest in his planet and culture and he'd felt pride that she was his lover.

She roused, a quiet snuffle and wriggle in his arms that brushed against his morning erection. He would love to take advantage of it, but knew time would be limited for the next few days. Regretfully he reached over and gently shook her shoulder. "Jessa?"

She snuffled again, rather sweetly, he thought and then she moved. "Wha...?"

His chest rumbled with laughter. "Jessa? It is time to rise."

She rolled. "What the...Galan?" Her face shone with a pink just-woken glow. "It wasn't a dream?" Her eyes sparkled, and he gloried in the sensation of being drawn to her.

"No. But if we don't hurry and prepare ourselves, we will be late. I believe it takes some of your hours to reach the base?"

"Yeah. It's over four hours by car." She moved quickly off the bed and he wished they had time together. But they didn't, so instead he rose and walked around to her. He stopped and smiled. "You forgot something."

Surprise shone on her face. "What did I forget?"

"To say good morning." He grinned her shock and dipped his mouth to hers. The kiss was chaste, but the passion remained, hovering just beyond reach.

They separated regretfully. He watched as Jessa snuck out of the room, grinning. *"Princess Gospah?"*

"Yes Galan?" The modulated voice filled the silence as the walls pulsed.

"Tell me when she is done and let her know I will meet her in the meal room. Also, if you can, please put her at ease. She is concerned that you would know when we are..." He didn't want to embarrass Jessa, but needed her to be comfortable in his world.

"When you are intimate? I will attempt to do so. Joras has also been wishful of contacting you. He says the escort has arrived and awaits."

He grimaced. This was not quite what he expected, but he was mindful of the strategic alliance this could form for both Hesparia and Earth. "Very well. Inform him that once Jessa and I have broken our fast we will leave with them."

"Very well." The pulsing of the walls ceased.

He hurried through his routine, dressing with care and placing a range of formal uniforms and tunics into a small bag together with other necessary items before hurrying to Jessa's door.

It opened at his command and he could see her, neatly folding clothing into a suitcase, a smaller packet sitting beside the pile of clothes. "You are nearly ready then?"

She jumped and turned, with a mock scowl. "Honestly Galan! You gave me a fright." Then she softened the words with a small smile before turning back to her packing, carefully placing the smaller item inside and fastening it. He reached out and grabbed it before she could.

"I can do that, you know."

"I know. But it's my pleasure to do little things for you." She blushed and he marveled at how her skin glowed. *It's such an endearing trait.* In fact, he nearly reached out for her, barely restraining the caress with a silent sigh. If they started, it would take time. They didn't exactly have a lot of that right now, so he waited until she closed her smaller bag and hefted it up over his shoulder with his own.

Together they left the room heading down the corridor toward the dining area.

THEY SETTLED into the big black car that had been waiting for them, and slowly pulled out of the facility. The chanting protestors were still there. This time when Jessa checked the faces in the crowd, she couldn't see any sign of Jace. She shrugged, wondering if her imagination was creating a problem that didn't exist, yet a seed of unease lodged in her mind. Determined to ignore the protestors, Jessa looked forward to the quiet time with Galan.

The sun had barely risen and for a while she watched the glorious colors emerging on the horizon—a montage of gold and pink streaking across the sky.

Joras and Seth travelled in the car behind them and each vehicle had two of the ship's security detail inside. That meant there was no real privacy to talk, so instead Jessa gazed at the changing landscape as the vehicle ate up the asphalt and the car hummed happily beneath them. For a while Galan worked on the tablet device and while Jessa wanted to know what he was doing, she was mindful that the driver could hear their every word. Instead she kept her counsel.

Every now and then, Galan would lightly touch her hand as if to check she was settled and comfortable. A happy warmth spread through her each time he did, and she'd turn away from the window to glance at his beloved face.

Muted mutterings also came from the front of the vehicle from both the driver and the security guard who travelled with them. No matter how much she strained, she could only catch the odd word. *Sedan. Following.* But she brushed the thoughts away as unimportant. Probably some kind of chatter about those in the convoy. After all, they were well protected.

Mile after mile passed by and Jessa wished for a book or even a magazine, wriggling a little as boredom ate at her. But she hadn't stashed one in her bag on that fateful day when she turned up to the observatory office, so she considered her options. In sheer desperation, Jessa fished her cell phone from her purse and turned it on, hunting for some inane game to play.

Galan glanced at her. "Do you need something?" He smiled and the ever-present warmth suffused her.

"No. I'm just looking for something to do." Her answer was little more than a breathy whisper. Once more she felt surprise at her own reaction to his simple smile.

He grinned and turned away. She hunted through the applications she had downloaded, finding a game that engaged her for some time. The endless stream of bricks moved around in order to make lines across the bottom of the screen without gaps. Galan looked at the screen and snickered.

Hearing the sound, she glanced up. "What?"

"Nothing." With a small laugh he turned back to his work and she sighed focusing back on her game finding that once more she'd been beaten. *I will find out why he laughed, later.*

After a while the phone beeped softly warning her it was low on battery power. She cursed under her breath, switched it off, watching as the screen turned black, then dropped the small device back to her bag. Jessa sighed and returned back to scanning the horizon, looking at the scrubby trees and grassland. After some time, an urgency in her bladder made itself known. "Umm, driver? Is there a rest stop somewhere around here?"

"Sure ma'am. There's one just ahead. We can stop there." His voice was strained, but she put it down to the long and tiring hours of travelling.

Jessa nodded and settled back into the seat, hoping it wouldn't take long to reach the point where they could locate a lavatory. The countryside had changed now, with rocky outcrops and small rivulets dotted here and there. The open woodland had been left far behind.

They drove through a small town and Jessa tapped her foot in a vain attempt to distract herself from the urgent call of nature. As they passed a big brick building the driver cursed, indicated his turn, and the vehicle made an arc across the asphalt. She was thrown against Galan, who righted her. As they drove back slowly, a convoy of trucks motored up the road, with the odd car interspersed between them.

"Do you need an escort Miss Bankia?" The security officer enquired with a slight smile on his face.

Jessa opened the door, grinned and shook her head. "No, I'm sure I'll be fine." With a quick scan of the road, left and right she scurried across the hot asphalt.

A small empty parking area faced the doorways at the back of the facility but she didn't pay a lot of attention, as the need was now extremely painful. Jessa hurried inside and took care of the task, washed her hands then rooted around in her handbag for a brush, lamenting the unkempt state of her hair. Unable to find one, she let out a small sigh and finger combed it, not wanting to look untidy in front of Galan. The sound of a vehicle pulling into the lot barely registered as she checked herself in the old tarnished mirror. Then she left the small facility, her bag slung over her arm. Her eyes downcast as she walked, looking only at the concrete path.

A thudding sound came from behind and she half turned, almost at the corner of the building. Something reach out smothering her mouth while an arm wrapped itself around her.

Jessa tried to scream and kicked out, striking flesh. An 'oomph' resonated and the whatever gripped her loosened, but not enough for her to escape.

A blow to the back of the head stole her senses and her vision turned black.

GALAN KNEW INSTANTLY that something was wrong. His chest ached, and a small gray vehicle screamed out of the parking area.

"Jessa!" He saw the car, which had entered after they'd stopped for Jessa's toilet break.

He wrenched the door open and looked quickly before crossing the now empty road. Sure enough, no sign of her existed except a few scuff marks and a small ear decoration. He hoped it was the one that didn't work, even as his stomach churned and his muscles clenched painfully.

Agent Foley came running as did Seth and Joras. "Where did

they go?"

"In the vehicle that just left." He shook off the rage. "I don't believe she went of her own accord." He held up the single earring, the communicator he'd sent to her. "I found this here."

Agent Foley looked stunned. "I... We didn't..." He shook his head. "*Damn.* We knew we were being followed, but we didn't expect —" Foley broke off, closing his eyes and Galan felt the punch of rage—at himself and at the agent in front of him. He ran his hands through his hair. He'd known that she was a target, but even he hadn't foreseen the danger in stopping at a public convenience. Galan damned himself as the pain inside his chest grew larger.

"Her phone!" Seth shouted, his eyes wild. "It has a GPS. Surely we can track her?"

For a moment a spark of hope shone brightly then dimmed within Galan. He shook his head. "She turned it off in the vehicle after it beeped at her." He rubbed his rib cage, trying to stave off the stabbing sensation, but it continued its growth, the ache spreading through his body. "We have to find her." His voice was harsher than usual, and he concentrated harder.

Joras looked at him, alarm clear in his eyes. "If we don't find her soon, you'll need a healer, right?"

Galan looked at him, saw the concern in his eyes and nodded. It was true. And if this was any indication, it would only get worse. They'd have to find her and soon.

Agent Foley pulled out his phone and started talking, sounding like a rapid tattoo as he gave directions. Then he listened and hung up. "We need to get to the cars."

He grasped Galan's arm and led him to the road verge. Galan let him lead the way, knowing he really should throw the man's hand off him. But he let it go. He didn't want to have that conversation right now. He just wanted Jessa back—safe and sound. They stumbled across the road and the guards climbed out, throwing themselves before him full of apologies, now that they'd grasped the gravity of the situation.

He raised a hand, cutting them off. "Not now. I just..." He turned away feeling the sting of tears. He refused to show a weakness before people he didn't trust. He was supposed to be a leader, yet right now, even that was stripped from him. "I just can't. Not now." He climbed into the vehicle and heard Joras ordering the guards to another car. Then Joras, Seth and Agent Foley followed him into the car with him. He breathed deeply, seeking control over his own emotions.

"Galan. We'll find her." Joras gazed at him steadily and Galan gave a single short nod.

Seth sat silently, fiddling with the tablet in his hands. Every now and again he would look up and when he caught Galan watching, would duck back down, touching his fingers to the screen.

"Seth? Do you have any idea of anyone who would want to hurt Miss Bankia?" Agent Foley's voice broke through the silence as the vehicle pulled onto the road once more.

"No. Why?" Seth looked up, his gaze shuttered.

Galan stared. *Where was this leading? What information did Foley have, that he, Galan, Heir of Hesparia, was unaware of?*

"She hasn't received any odd communications since you became involved in the negotiations?"

"Well... the media outlets have been emailing... and her family are really mad at her. People seem to think she's sold out to the aliens. Apart from that, no." He hesitated, slightly. "Well..." His voice died away, and his facial expression changed to horror. "Only... Well, only Jace. But I doubt..."

Agent Foley picked up his phone, dialed and once more spoke in rapid sentences. "What is his last name and where does he live?"

Galan watched Seth's face show bewilderment. "Geez... how would I know? I doubt even Aunt Veronica knows where he lives." He shrugged awkwardly in the enclosed space.

"Can you contact your aunt?" Galan perched in the seat, hopeful that they could deal with this quickly and that the woman would tell him where Jessa was. Reassure him that all was well.

"I don't have her number, but my mother would." He put the tablet down on his knees and fished in a pocket, pulling out a phone and dialed.

Galan rubbed his chest again as Seth tried. "It's engaged. I can try again in a few minutes."

Each minute seemed to last forever, and Galan hated the help-less frustration that churned within him. Thoughts of Jessa dead, hurt or even *bodily damaged* ran through his mind, teasing him with presentiments of the ugliest actions he'd encountered on his own and other planets. *What if I never see her again?* His stomach roiled at the thought, but he attempted vainly to shrug them off.

The car kept travelling and Seth tried again. This time he was successful and gave them a thumbs up signal as he started talking. "Hey Mum? Can I have Aunt Veronica's number?" His expression looked pained. "Yeah… yeah… look… I know. Yes, I will. No, I won't." Then he tucked the phone between his shoulder and cheek and picked up the tablet, rapidly tapping down a series of numbers. "Yeah. Thanks Mum."

He rang off. "Here's Aunt Veronica's number." He handed over the tablet and stashed the phone back into his shirt.

Just as he did Galan's communicator started vibrating. *Could it be? Jessa?* He depressed the button.

"*Galan? Are you there?*" The voice was little more than a whisper but Galan had never heard anything so fantastic or welcomed before.

"Jessa? Where are you?"

"I think I'm in the boot of a car. It's travelling fast. I just don't know which way." Her voice was shaky, and rage consumed him once more.

He bottled it and kept his mind on asking questions that would reassure him and help them to locate her. "Are you okay? You aren't hurt?"

"I have a devil of a headache from when he hit me with some-thing. So, I'm sore. Apart from that, though, I'm unharmed. I think." She grunted, and a tinny sound came over the small device.

"Tell her to turn on her phone," Seth interrupted.

"I heard that. Let me see if I can find it. It's dark and hot in here." He could hear the panic in her voice. Small rustling sounds filled his hearing and then an "Aha! Tell him I've turned it on, but I only have limited battery."

Agent Foley started talking into his phone once again.

"Wait, they're slowing down. Oh God! I think we're stopping. I have to hang up now, otherwise he might find it. I'll stick it in my underwear though."

"Shit! We just need another couple of seconds. Tell her to leave it on." Agent Foley cried from the front seat. "Damn! We got a partial location. Somewhere in Orange. Near Moulder Street. It's bouncing off the network there."

"Hang on Jessa, we have an idea where you are."

But she didn't answer, and the scorch of frustration ate at him again. *Soon.* Soon they would get her back and he'd make sure the ones who took her, paid for their mistake.

JESSA HASTILY STASHED the cell down her bra, wriggling madly as the boot opened. She looked up into the sunlight and was blinded.

She felt hands on her, gripping her tight and she pulled against them. "Let me go!"

"I don't think so Jessa." She stilled, surprised by the voice. She knew that voice very well.

Jace.

"Damn it, what in *hell* do you think you're doing Jace Dentrix?"

He stood her up and she glared at him. "I don't want to be anywhere near you. Now take me back."

He snickered and as her vision cleared she saw the flash of teeth and the perfectly groomed blond hair. But the lines and hollows of his face told her he hadn't aged well in the years since she'd last seen him.

"Let's talk inside." He attempted to steer her inside an old building, but she fought against him, pulling away. "Come on Jessa, I really don't want to hurt you." But he already was. The pain in her chest was excruciating and growing stronger each moment.

Jace gripped her hand once more and she tugged, breaking free. She turned only to find two big and burly men waiting for her.

"Jace? What are you going to do to me?" Her voice quivered and for the first time, true fear intruded and she stepped back into Jace's arms. "Let me go and I won't tell anyone." She pleaded but was disheartened when he laughed and hauled her to the structure, then pushed her inside.

The interior of the hall was almost empty, but she spied rows of chairs and a doorway at the back. A glance behind told her that the men had followed them inside and she shivered, knowing their presence didn't bode well for her.

Jace let go of her and she pulled her hands close to her body, rubbing on the wrist that had taken the majority of the abuse.

"Now come through to the back and I'll make you a cup of tea. That is what you still drink, isn't it?" He sneered at her. Anger spurted through her veins. Why should he deride her? She wasn't the one who'd done the wrong thing for years. She was the one with a chance for a bright new future, not him. Not for one moment did she trust him, so Jessa shook her head. The ache in her skull reminded her of the damage he'd done to her. Reality intruded. To get out of this mess, she'd do whatever it took. "No thank you. But I would prefer to find the bathroom, so I can inspect the damage you did to me."

"Jessa, Jessa. Honestly, if you hadn't fought me, it wouldn't have been necessary."

Her skin crawled at his reasonable tone. *Seriously, what weed is he smoking these days to act as if his actions were reasonable?* "Bathroom, please Jace." She needed to get away. A plan formed in her mind as he indicated through the doorway.

"It's out the back." He smiled, and she wanted to cringe away from the look in his eyes. "And Jessa? You can't escape. One of my helpers, Faith is waiting out there for you. She'll escort you into the bathroom."

Jessa wanted to scream, but so long as Faith didn't follow her into the stall, at least she could follow through on her plan. She moved slowly. It wouldn't do to make Jace any more suspicious than he already was.

Once through the doorway she saw the woman, waiting for her.

Her long blonde hair tied up in a messy bun away from her face, with tiny wisps escaping. Her dress, a shabby floral affair was both shapeless and long, covering her all the way to her ankles and her feet were shod in sensible slip-on brown shoes. Everything about his dowdy follower screamed plain and unadorned. Downtrodden. There was no way Jessa allow that to happen to her.

Faith rose and edged closer. "Greetings Jessa. Jace informed us that you would be joining us for the meeting and afterwards for a detoxification session. Now, I suppose you would like to prepare yourself? I have arranged a dress and shoes for you. After all, those worldly trappings you wear will be a barrier to accepting the truth." Faith smiled and indicated to the side and wide eyed, Jessa walked forward and opened the door. Two stalls were in the room and she thanked whatever was on her side for that small mercy.

Faith came closer. "I will wait here for you and then you can change." She picked a shapeless brown dress up off the single wooden chair that sat in the corner.

Jessa wanted to yell at Faith but refrained and retreated within the stall, latching it firmly then pulled the phone from her bra. She muffled it carefully within the folds of her clothes making as much noise with the toilet roll holder and one hand to cover the sounds. Once the phone logged onto the network, she switched it to silent. They should be able to find her so long as the phone didn't beep or the battery gave out. She propped it behind the bent pipes within the piles of dust she found there.

Surely they would be able to find the location with that?

Then she flushed, making out she had used the facilities before she exited the stall.

Faith waited while she washed her hands and pushed the dress at her.

"You know Faith, I rather like what I'm wearing right now." She needed to keep Jace's follower focused on her, not on the stall she had just left.

Faith looked at Jessa with consternation. "But they're far too worldly."

"I like them."

Faith tsk tsk'ed. "Jace did say you had been tainted by the alien. We'll just have to show you the truth." She advanced.

Jessa stepped away.

"Ladies? I will need your assistance." At those words another door at the end opened and three women entered the bathroom.

"Get your clothes off please." The biggest woman of the trio made the request and Jessa had the disquieting thought that if she didn't, they would strip her anyway.

Slowly she began to remove her slacks, regretful because they were her favorite. Then came her blouse in a pretty floral print. They exclaimed that at least below it all she had sensible taste in underwear, and the sense of violation leached into Jessa, fed by the comments of the women surrounding her. Angry tears stung her eyes, but she followed the requests, not wanting to know what retribution might be enacted on her.

Faith thrust the ugly gown at Jessa who grimaced but pulled it over her head and slid her feet into the nondescript brown slip on shoes.

"Take off the earrings and necklace please." Faith held out a hand.

"No. I won't." *Oh God!* That was her last link to Galan. Her stomach quivered, and her heart pounded. This time when the ache hit her chest, she groaned. Her stomach ready to release its contents as the pain overwhelmed her. "Oh...I'm going to be sick." They backed away hastily and Jessa ran for the stall, making the toilet in time to throw up.

GALAN HEARD JESSA. *Jace Dentrix.* Damn the bastard that was Seth's cousin. She'd acted quickly in turning on the phone and stashing it. He heard the comment "I don't really want to hurt you" and his rage grew to incandescence. If he could have laid his hands on the man... Then he heard the fear in her voice. He balled his hands while he ground his teeth together. If they hurt her... There would be nowhere in the galaxy that would be safe from his wrath.

"Be calm Galan. We will find her." Joras intoned calmly but nothing could settle the turmoil and pain. Agent Foley was making quick calls and giving instructions to the crew while he broadcast the conversation to the others. Thankfully his security officers had shown her how to mute the communicator so their contact was one way.

Then he heard the woman's voice and his skin crawled. "What is going on?" He looked to Agent Foley and saw the shuttered look on his face, but the tic at the corner of his mouth gave away his agitation.

"Who is this man? What does he want with Jessa?" Galan demanded.

Foley spoke quickly into the phone then turned to give the driver directions ending with "Go faster."

He didn't handle not being in command well, Galan discovered. "Tell me now." He turned back to Seth. "Tell me everything."

Seth shrank into the corner. "Let me ring my mother and we'll see what she can tell me." Seth made the phone call, asking about what Jace was doing. Who he associated with. Where he lived. With each answer he paled and finally hung up. "Oh man. He's joined a cult. Somewhere in Orange. Mum isn't sure where, but apparently Aunt Veronica doesn't have an address, she rang her after I spoke with her. All she said is that he thought her too worldly and she wouldn't convert, he wanted nothing to do with her." Seth shrugged. "Sorry Galan. I tried."

"Got it!" Agent Foley called from the front seat. Galan sat up, listening to the sounds of Jessa being violently ill. His own stomach churned wildly, and he swallowed the bile that rose in his throat. "We had the state police on stand-by and we're sending them in. They should be surrounding the building about now."

The vehicle screamed down the road. Galan worried, hearing the shouts that now emanated through the communicator. "Stay still! This is the police."

"You bitch! How did you tip them off?" The vitriol in the voice turned his blood cold. He willed the vehicle to move faster as they raced into the town and down a street. The small flag on the front of the car flapped as they careened madly.

Then he heard crashing and banging. Women shouted and the demands to lie down on the floor. *I should have kept her safe.*

"Officer, my name is Jessa Bankia." He heard her tremulous words and nearly broke down, knowing she was once more safe, though not yet in his arms. The car slowed and he demanded to know why from the driver.

"This is it. Let's go get your girl." Foley answered as he flung open the door. An officer made a move to stop them, then saw the flags adorning the front of the vehicle, his eyes widened before he started backing away.

"Inside, Sir." The young man indicated with a shaking hand to a wooden door on a building a little way down the street. Agent Foley hurried away with the rest of his men following closely behind.

They moved through the milling people. Every now and then someone challenged them. Agent Foley took point, dealing with them using terse language and his commanding presence while Galan searched the room for Jessa. A bunch of women were ushered through by others in blue uniforms.

Finally, there was Jessa. Her face blotchy and her eyes damp. She must have seen him because she smiled tremulously and ran towards him, halting as another officer blocked and waylaid her.

She struggled. Her face now set. "Let me through."

Galan growled. *No one treats Jessa like that.* The thought bloomed, and he advanced only to find his way blocked by Agent Foley.

The officer responded with a short answer and she stopped. She looked at him and he saw the glint of fury in her eyes.

Agent Foley grabbed Galan by the arm. "Let me deal with this." But Jessa was already arguing in low hissing tones. Galan waited as Foley waved a badge at the officer in blue. A quick discussion took place then Jessa moved towards Galan.

When she reached him, she sobbed angrily. He enfolded her in his arms, uncaring of who saw them together. She rubbed the back of her head, breathing roughly as if in pain and he let go. "You need a healer."

"I think I just might." Then her eyes rolled back in their sockets as she slumped to the floor.

JESSA'S HEAD hurt like blazes. She moaned slightly, squinting against the annoying bright lights. She lifted her hand, feeling Galan's fingers which moved over her head. But no matter how gentle or soft they were, the touch still hurt as he checked over her skull.

"Oww." She complained weakly.

The sound was met by a watery chuckle. The voice she was pretty sure she knew.

"Jessa. My Jessa. You scared me so much. You will never be allowed anywhere by yourself now."

Galan. Yes, he was here and she was safe. Scenes from before the blackout rose in her mind and she shivered. She opened her eyes to see him leaning over her and smiled. Another quick glance showed her lying on the seat of the car with her head cradled in Galan's lap as others huddled around the open door. "Oh I need…" She rose up and a moment of vertigo saw her sink back down. Her stomach jostled and she regretted the action.

"Jessa, you should lie still for a while."

She nodded carefully, noting how the pain in her chest and head had abated, unlike the weird sensations that she still experienced, such as her stomach rising into her throat. "The healer has seen you, but he thought it best that you rest still for a little longer." Galan hugged her closer. Jessa soaked up the comfort before attempting to push him away. She had no intentions of causing a scene.

"Galan!" Her voice was a little stronger than before, but the thud and thump continued to reverberate in her head.

He grinned tightly. "It's all right. We are among friends." He pushed her back to his lap with soft hands.

"Sure. Fine .I'll lie down again too." She closed her eyes as she settled her head onto his lap, only to open them seconds later. "My phone! Where is it?" Agitation flowed through her. *Where was her phone?*

"We haven't found it yet." She could feel the vibrations of Galan's words.

"I hid it. Behind one of the toilets in the ladies room." She could see Agent Foley nodding and as he made to move she flung out a hand. "While you are there, could you please retrieve my clothes? I would prefer them to this." She grabbed a handful of the dowdy cloth in disgust.

The agent smiled and retreated without a word.

"So, you obviously found me well enough."

He nodded silently.

She smiled. "Did you get Jace too? I didn't see him in the room when you arrived."

"He got away." Galan's face tightened. "No one seems to know how."

She sighed. "So, as you were saying. How will you protect me, even in the ladies room?"

Galan smiled tightly. "That is easy. The team has arranged for a female security guard to travel with us. She will meet us in Rich Mond?"

Jessa sputtered a laugh at his pronunciation of Richmond but didn't correct it.

"After this, there will be no chances taken with your safety."

Closing her eyes, she rested against him. How much more difficult would it make the situation, she wondered.

"Apart from the head injury… You were unharmed?" He seemed hesitant.

She sighed. "Yeah. Humiliated. Embarrassed. But that is the worst of the injuries I received."

He shuddered and she understood his concern. "No! Oh heavens, Galan. No one touched me like that." She sat up and turned, resting a hand against his cheek, waiting for the world to stop spinning. "I would tell you. Truly, I am fine."

He folded his arms around her. "Then my world is right again."

Chapter 8

Jessa shook in the cold air. They'd finally arrived at the air force base, taking off a good five hours after their appointed time. Galan had been solicitous, keeping her by his side until summoned away. When the female agent, Danni McCall had joined them, he'd given her strict instructions that Jessa's safety was of priority to him. The Prime Minister quirked a brow at the comment before dragging him away to discuss tactics and personalities. Jessa reclined, watching while all the agents sat to the back, companionably chatting away. Seth also managed to find someone to talk to, sitting opposite Joras and discussing algorithms. She noticed the glances he sent in Agent McCall's direction, even though he was attempting to be discreet.

The agent was young looking, with a short black bob. Of average height perhaps, but there was a fierceness in her eyes that made Jessa blink more than once. Her brown eyes were hard in her small pixie face, which seemed to marry with her whipcord lean figure while exuding strength and determination. But she'd been friendly enough, so Jessa smiled at the introduction and continued to watch her.

A shiver wracked her body, and a touch on her shoulder surprised Jessa. She jumped.

Galan frowned. "Jessa? Are you cold?" His swift motion forward nearly overwhelmed her as his arms folded once more around her.

"Yes… No…" Confusion set in. Just what did she feel? *Sadness? Fear? Loneliness?* She looked up to see him scowling and a hostess moved to attend him.

"Captain Galan? Is there something I can do for you?" She smiled at him and Jessa nearly rolled her eyes.

"Jessa is cold. We need a blanket and warm drinks."

The woman smiled and strode away purposefully. Galan found the empty seat beside her and settled in, drawing her close against him. She savored the warmth of his body. The subtly erotic scent emanating from him acted as a sedative for her overwrought system.

The fear she'd ruthlessly suppressed bubbled to the surface as another shiver wracked her body. Jessa squeezed her eyes shut. A single fat tear escaped and rolled down her face, burning itself onto her cold skin.

"You're safe now, Jessa." He pulled her closer and she burrowed in, closing her eyes and seeking the strength she could only draw from him.

"I was so scared." Her words wavered, and she wanted to swallow them back. Yet there was no containing the racking sobs. Galan appeared to understand her fears and concerns, rocking her back and forth. Time slowed and dragged out while she was lost in her misery. Gradually the mists of the negative emotions left her. Jessa became aware of the blanket around her shoulders and the way he rubbed her back, a slow up and down caress which relaxed her.

"It's okay. You needed to let it go." His quietly whispered words were meant to be reassuring, but instead reminded her of how she had fallen apart on him. It wasn't the look she wanted him to see.

Jessa pulled away, scrubbing at her face. "I shouldn't have lost it like that."

He sighed. "Jessa, you've had a really difficult few days. It's okay to feel hurt, dismayed, frightened and even concerned about the dangers you've already encountered. It doesn't make you seem any less capable in my eyes." He stopped and put a finger under her chin, pushing it up so that she looked into his eyes. "It just tells me that you have softness where it counts but can still be strong when you need to be." He bent his head until he pressed his lips against hers, the brief touch reinforcing his words.

A sigh escaped as he gently pulled away. "Shame we're here..." She let the words trail away.

He chuckled. "Maybe, but we have some work to do right now." She looked at him. *Work?*

He reached for her hand and holding it tight, tugged her to the meeting table area where she had seen other people congregating earlier. This time, Joras and Seth waited for them and she found herself smiling even as she continued wiping at her face.

Seth stood and came over, eyeing Galan off before he opened his arms. Jessa found herself in a hug. "I'm so pleased you're okay, Jessa. Jace should never have done what he did." Seth's earnest voice nearly set off another spate of tears, but she bit her lip, letting the pain battle her ragged feelings into some form of submission.

Joras smiled, one that reached his eyes as he held out a hand. "I am pleased you are back and unharmed."

Then they sat down, talking about what they needed to achieve with the United Nations.

"So, then. What do we do next?" Seth sat upright in his seat. "You have a plan of attack and Joras and I have worked out how we can display the images of Hesparia through a data projector. Joras reckons he could take some doctors back to Hesparia to show them how to heal others." He was so earnest sitting there, that she wanted to smile and pat him on the head. Instead she restrained herself to grinning at his boyish enthusiasm.

A meal was delivered to the table by the new agent, Danni McCall. Jessa watched, amused as Seth quieted, becoming both thoughtful and charming in her presence. She made a note to discuss it with Galan later, noting the faint blush and shine in the eyes of the agent every time she looked at Seth. A budding romance was what she saw before her. Maybe even possible life partners... another couple to repopulate Hesparia, she thought, before stopping herself. That was the sort of pressure he probably didn't need at the moment.

TOUCHING down in New York was a revelation to the crewmembers of the *Princess Gospah*. Officials entered the plane in order to process their entry into the United States and Galan watched bemused at the to-ing and fro-ing that took place. Only the members of his crew were immune from the customs routine. But that didn't include Seth or Jessa. Specialist agents from the Department of Homeland Security and the Diplomatic Security Services entered the plane while others waited below at the vehicles and steps.

When they checked Jessa's details, faces were pulled and a huddle ensued. Galan watched, the muscles in his face tightening as he thought over the facts as he knew them. She had made a mistake when she was younger and judging by the murmurs and shaking heads she was about to be made to pay again.

Not while she's with me. He tensed as an older man moved in his direction.

Galan watched the man look at Jessa then back to him. Jessa's face was red and her eyes teary. "Captain Galan… Sir… We have to refuse your companion entry into the United States. She has a criminal record."

"I am here as part of the diplomatic mission for the Hesparian's." She countered with a quiet dignity. But he could clearly see the crimson tide staining her cheeks and the way she shook.

His anger rose. "Her presence is not negotiable to me. Either Jessa Bankia is with me, or I do not enter your country." He sat himself down on the seat. He knew the political ramifications of his actions. And frankly, right now, he didn't care. If Jessa wasn't with him, he'd be beside himself the whole time she was absent. A little political leverage at this point might just hold sway, he told himself.

"Sir. I don't think you understand…" The man looked earnestly at him and Galan glared back infusing his eyes with all his ire which had built within him. The man backed away and started conferring once more with his counterparts.

Jessa moved scooting along one of the bench seats by the open door, until she leaned against him. "Galan, don't give this up for me. I'll be fine."

He knew she wouldn't be. Couldn't be. He placed his arm around her shoulder. "Wait and see what happens." He continued watching the urgent discussions across the cabin noting that one left the craft with his cell device against his ear. He controlled the grin that he knew would break over his face if he let it, aware that wouldn't help his cause. He glanced at Joras and Seth and his security team, their huddle at the other end of the plane showing their discomfort with whatever was happening. Even the Prime Minister had left her office and frowned unhappily at the situation.

"Captain Galan..." He raised a hand and looked to Jessa as he refused the easy option of leaving Jessa behind.

Finally the customs officer who'd left earlier returned, whispering furiously with the rest. They shook heads and one shrugged before he advanced towards himself and Jessa. Once he understood their intentions, amusement filled Galan.

"After checking with our central office, it has been determined that we will allow Miss Bankia entry. However, should there be any issues, the temporary entry visa will be revoked immediately." He looked at Jessa and once more Galan's ire rose at the expression of menace on the man's face.

Jessa laid a hand on Galan's wrist. "Fine. I understand fully." She cleared her throat, the heat in her skin scorching him as they rose together and made their way closer to the open door of the airplane. He didn't really understand but shrugged it off. Right now as Jessa was once more free to travel with his entourage, he needed to focus on the task ahead. The Prime Minister had already made it clear she couldn't give any guarantee of assistance to himself or the cause, given they were talking not just migration within their planet, but off world.

She'd also pressed for special favors including trading agreements and diplomatic missions. Something he couldn't presently agree to, until he knew what other offers would be made and he'd stated that to her dismay. She'd been most unhappy then recollected that he would be under her auspices, as if that alone gave her some sort of cachet. He shrugged and let her continue to think that. It suited his purposes for now.

A sound at the doorway drew his attention and he noted that the Prime Minister stood waving before a range of flashing lights. He looked to Jessa. "What is going on?"

She smiled. "It's called a media scrum. There are lots of journalists taking photos of this momentous occasion. That is why there are so many waiting for you. Australia doesn't usually have this kind of reception, from what I understand, so I guess she's making hay while the sun shines."

Galan frowned. *When else would you make hay except during the daylight hours? And what did that have to do with the Prime Minister?* "I don't understand."

"What?"

"What does the making of hay have to do with our arrival?"

Jessa blinked then sighed. "Sure, you don't understand that." He turned, savoring the glinting of reflected light he saw in her eyes. "Well, she's taking advantage of the opportunity this presents to increase her profile. But that will only last until you make it to the door. Then you will be the one they want to see." She smiled and stepped away seeing the Prime Minister holding out her hand. "Go on and join her. I'll stay with Joras and Seth and the rest of the team until we catch up."

That isn't going to happen... His mind argued with his heart. He didn't want to leave her behind, but he was here on a mission. The mission had to take center stage, if they had any hopes of repopulating and saving his planet. He nodded his reluctant agreement and moved to stand beside the female at the door. She gripped his hand, raising it above their heads and smiled broadly.

"Smile, Captain Galan. This is a moment of triumph."

But to him, without Jessa by his side it was empty. Finally they were allowed to walk down the steps, and the bustle of staff behind him followed. He glanced over his shoulder to see Jessa and Seth surrounded by his team and her security guard as they followed him to a vehicle. He was ushered within the front one and the door shut as they sped away.

JESSA WATCHED as the car Galan had got into sped toward the gate. She knew he hadn't left her behind on purpose. Understood it was part of the grandstanding that the Prime Minister would use for jockeying for position. No, it was part of the way things were done. But it didn't make her feel any less unhappy with the situation.

They were ushered to the waiting cars, and climbed in, Joras and Seth together with herself and Danni and a couple of the security detail shared one vehicle while others got into similar black people movers. The car pulled out and tucked in behind Galan's. Police outriders met them at the sliding gates and they were on the road. She glanced out of the darkly tinted windows, the now familiar sight of protestors with placards chanting and jeering making her cringe a little. The conveyance moved slowly into the main traffic then gathered speed.

Their trip was quick and as night fell she had the impression of a smoother ride and better roads than at home. The trip itself didn't take long until they pulled up outside an elegant hotel. The entrance was brightly lit and a major-domo in resplendent livery opened the door once they drew up under the portico. Inside the hotel though, the red furnishings and flash of bulbs overwhelmed her. Security guards swarmed the lobby, forming a human chain for the distinguished visitors to make their way to the end of the open foyer.

The security services had already checked them in apparently and hustled them into the waiting elevators they had appropriated for the duration of their stayed in the hotel. Galan had obviously dug his heels in, waiting for her and his face creased into a smile when he saw her. She hurried to him and took his hand while the click click of bulbs left Jessa momentarily deaf as he ushered her into the small box. Then it shut and merciful silence descended once more.

In the corner, Jessa could see the Prime Minister, her face sober for an instant as she watched them together, scanning the way Galan held her against him. "Well then, I suppose we had better ensure your bags are conveyed to the captain's room," she grated. The elevator stopped and with a silent gesture they were ushered into the corridor.

The manager waited for them to move in their direction, trolleys loaded with ice buckets, wine and fruit baskets stood beside him. "Prime Minister. Welcome. Come this way." He ushered her into a room. "We have attended to all the details. The room has been inspected and the floors above and below have been cleared for your teams." He picked up a basket of fruit, pressing it into her hands. Deftly, she handed it to one of her security team who had obviously come up in another elevator and slipped in behind her. They placed it on the table beside the door in silence.

"Thank you."

The manager grinned and pushed in the cart loaded with goodies while the Prime Minister waited. A mask of interest settled on her face and slowly she moved him out the door. Jessa and Galan followed him.

The manager then looked at Galan. "Captain. This is such an honor." He bowed low showing the slightly balding center of his salt and pepper hair. "Let me escort you to your rooms." He led them down the corridor, all obsequious attention and opened the door to another luxurious suite. The cream papers on the wall teamed with dark wood, merging happily with the reds of the draperies and gilt work. They followed him within and he pointed out the comforts they could enjoy. Jessa bit her tongue. Never before had she stayed in a room so lushly furnished.

The manager helpfully moved to the large doors and with a flourish opened them to display a balcony with a view of Central Park. The wispy curtains flew in the breeze and she shivered as a touch of colder air caressed her skin. Jessa clutched both arms around herself, hoping he would soon be gone and she could close the windows.

Once more a cart was wheeled in and baskets of fruit, chocolates and champagnes were dispensed while they waited. His effusive offers of anything they wanted continued as they herded him in the direction of the door. Even as he entered the corridor, Jessa spied Danni, Seth and Joras making their way into rooms across from their suite and smiled. "At least we'll all be within shouting distance."

Galan made a noise of agreement as he shut the door behind the manager.

"How do I lock this?" Even as he turned back to her, his eyes glittered with erotic promise. She moved to engage the locks and turned to find him pushing closed the windows to the balcony. Then she moved, stepping into his open and waiting arms.

He leaned in to kiss her. The slow unhurried pace of his lips warming her from within as his tongue sought and gained entry. She moaned low in her throat and he deepened the caress, while he cupped her buttocks…

The knock at the door had them springing apart. "I will kill…"

Jessa laughed and stepped away. "Let me check the door." She peered through the small peep hole and saw a doorman, pushing a trolley piled with their bags. "It's just one of the staff. Let me get that."

She opened the door as the man stepped inside.

GALAN CAUGHT sight of the glint below the white cloth on the other man's arm and pushed Jessa out of the way. She gasped and fell against the wall. "Galan? What are you…"

The waiter lifted two hands, his face a pasty white. "Hey man… I'm just delivering the bags and a corkscrew…" He backed away from them.

Jessa sighed. "It's okay Galan. I'll get this." Her soft voice told him that he'd overreacted. But in the name of the goddess, after she'd been abducted he saw dangerous thoughts and actions towards her in every person's gaze. He'd seen the quiet strength in her, yet the primal core of him needed to protect his mate. Even travelling to the hotel, he'd worried until he'd seen her again. No matter that she had a guard, he needed to see her in order to be assured of her safety. He knew it was foolish, pushing her like that. The glint had reminded him of a knife…and he'd just…well, he'd just acted. *Foolishly.*

He turned away listening to Jessa's voice smoothing over the incident. From the corner of his eye he could see the man carrying their small bags and depositing them next to the big bed. Finally, the door shut and he turned.

"Jessa… I…"

She moved into his arms, wrapping hers around his waist. "I understand Galan. But not everyone is going to try to hurt us. To take away what we have."

He breathed deeply, inhaling the scent of her, letting it fill his senses.

"Now, I doubt they are going to want to meet with us tonight. It's what? Eight o'clock here? Let's grab some food and head to bed." She smiled and his stomach warmed, the curl of pleasure moved through his insides until he was full of heat. He nodded.

She grinned. "Let me see what's available from room service." She moved to the large desk and picked up the folder, leafing through. "How hungry are you?"

Galan thought, he really wasn't, given the meals that had been delivered on board the plane. "Not overly."

She concentrated on the menu and he watched her. The way the tip of her pink tongue emerged at the corner of her lips reminded him of her luscious taste. It tantalized and teased until he couldn't wait any longer. She turned to put down the folder as he moved in behind her.

"Forget the food. That's not what I'm hungry for." He slipped his hands over the twin mounds of her breasts. Her breath caught, he could hear the ragged cadence and it made him harder and hotter. Ready for Jessa.

She covered his hands with her own as she dropped her head back with a low moan. "Oh Galan. I've missed your touch over the last two days."

Her words were the final straw as he whirled her to face him. "Then show me." His guttural words echoed through the room as he kissed her, devouring her lips and diving within the warm cavern of her mouth.

Tasting.

Plundering.

Demanding.

He felt her pluck at the closure of his jacket while he sought the button and zip, quickly dispensing with them and pushing the pants from her hips.

Now.

"Here."

He needed to sink himself into her welcoming body. To feel the heat of her skin against his. To plunder her and feel the life affirming bond they shared.

She pulled her mouth away. "Bedroom…" Her breathless entreaty was lost as he burrowed his fingers beneath her plain white panties and she gasped as he hooked at the edges and shoved them down.

"Now. Here." His demand was met by her pushing the shirt from his shoulders and then she found his pants, fumbling while he watched, amazed and humbled at the beauty of this woman who wanted him as much as he wanted her. The tide of pink on her skin told him of her growing arousal as did the shine in her eyes.

She pushed the material away and found the drawstring of his under things, deftly tugging then they too fell to the floor. Then he hissed as the cool air found his overheated skin. His erection was ready for her, for the scalding heat he knew he'd find within her body. Unable to wait, he lifted her to the desk and steadied her on the wood surface, then he gripped her hips tightly.

He looked into her eyes, saw she was as aroused now as he was. Then he dropped to his knees before her, parted her legs. Her sex quivered and he reached for her. "All for me."

Jessa scootched to the edge and quickly dispensed with the panties that tangled at her ankles. Unable to wait he bent forward parting her legs further so he could gaze upon her most intimate flesh. It glistened in the light, swollen and damp. Ready for him.

He leaned in and she shivered. "Galan? Please." He devoured Jessa with a quick upward stroke she shuddered and cried out. The taste…so musky and essentially *her* filled his senses. He had to have more. He moved again and she moaned and arched into his ministrations. He undulated faster and wilder as she squirmed and ached, cried and keened. Each taste more fulfilling than the last and soon he fastened his lips over her, suckling at her.

With a single high pitched keen she came and he exulted. This was his woman. He stood, positioning himself between her parted thighs, unable to contain his need further and a single swift move thrust him home, embedding himself within her swollen flesh. Her sweet sex surrounded him, welcoming him. He surged, riding the aftermath of her climax as she shuddered.

He grazed his fingers over her, rubbing and arousing, tearing at her shirt so he could bare her glorious breasts. "For me. You will come for me. With me."

He pulled the material from her shoulders, tore at her bra which ripped under his demanding hands while he rocked within her. Back and forth each movement heightening his sensations while his heart thundered in his chest.

Jessa wound her legs around his waist and he knew the instant the fever was upon her again as she strained to him. "Galan. Galan. Galan," She chanted his name, each time lower and more needy than the last. She gripped him with her thighs like a vice as she held onto him.

And this time, together they found their climax.

JESSA SHOOK.

In the aftermath of their wild lovemaking she wobbled to the bathroom as Galan trailed behind her, her mind whirling. *How could it be so wild and yet tender unless it is love?* Sure, he'd told her about the *Quickening*, but she'd taken that with a huge grain of salt. But the need that had flared within her for him, the way he'd loved her... The memory of it had her breath stuttering in her chest.

Could she have really fallen for him? The instant that thought occurred she knew the answer. She had. *I've fallen for the sexiest alien. One who will leave.* One who said he'd take her with him, but she couldn't be totally sure.

Even now, as she blindly groped for the door to the shower he was there. Her eyes burned, but she wouldn't give in to that particular weakness. He hadn't said the words, but given the way they had come together... surely he must feel something for her? Apart from the biological connection the *Quickening* obviously wrought on their systems?

"Jessa?" He must have seen the tension in her shoulders. "Are you all right?"

I can't turn around. I can't let him see me like this. I won't embarrass myself or him with this show of unwelcome emotion.

"Sure. Yeah." Her words were husky with unshed tears. *How can I face him?*

"Jessa?"

She turned the water on and dashed under it. Hoping it would hide her tears. But nothing could stop the turmoil in her head. She knew it wasn't because of the *Quickening*. It was the real thing. She ached to tell him. But she couldn't. Not until she knew if he felt the same. *No, definitely not*, her brain answered. But she could show him and hope he would eventually feel the same way. So Jessa reached out a hand, gazing at him. He looked at her. A question shimmered in his eyes. Then he reached out and took her hand, moved into the stall with her.

"Love me again." Her urgent demand was met with a slow smile. It spread across his face and his eyes glittered once again.

"Here?" He spread his hands indicating the small enclosure.

"Yes. Now." She moved, stretching her hands out to him. "Here and now."

She sank to her knees before him. He smiled. It was wicked and filled her with warmth. She studied him. His body was perfectly formed. Not too much hair. The berry brown making her skin look so much whiter against his and she could see where she started and he ended. That turned her on. So much more than she ever thought it would.

The water pounded on her head as she circled his ankles with her fingers. She rubbed them lightly, enjoying the feel of bones beneath his skin as the water played over her sensitized body. She trailed her hands up over his legs to his knees, so perfectly formed in her opinion. She slid her hands along his skin and let them glide up his thighs. He hissed as she gently played. Jessa touched him with feather light movements inching to his inner thighs. Galan groaned lightly and moved his legs a little.

His erection was at the right height and she swayed forward. Opened her mouth and took it in. Curled her tongue around the velvety hardness and heard his groan of pleasure.

"What you do to me, Jessa."

She swayed slowly, back and forth and clasped her hands on his hips. Felt the bones beneath her touch and the locked muscles. He rocked slightly and she gloried. She might be all his, but he was also all hers.

She sucked harder while he caught her hair in his hand. She ran her tongue down the underneath of his shaft. Each movement wringing another groan or moan from his mouth and she glanced up, she dug her nails into his backside, holding him firmly against her. His eyes were closed and he breathed heavily.

She released him long enough to whisper. "Turnabout is fair play, Galan." Then once more she closed her lips around him.

He pushed in, surging closer, undulating against her mouth, meeting each long draw with a gentle thrust.

Faster. He moved a little faster and she sucked a little harder, letting her tongue work on him. "Jessa…" His moans turned her on. Her own body now tightly wound once more. Each small droplet of water that passed over her nipples exquisite torture and her core ached with emptiness. It wasn't enough. She needed more. She needed Galan. She needed him embedded within her. She opened her mouth and released his engorged flesh.

Galan swooped down to the floor. "You are bedeviling me." He thrust his hand between her legs as the other fondled her breast, she squirmed against his erotic invasion. Galan slipped one finger inside, not enough to satisfy and she cried out. "More Galan. I need more."

He chuckled. "Not yet." He slipped the single digit out and between her sensitive folds.

She keened in her throat as he laved the outline of her ear. "I hear this can be quite an erogenous zone." Just the merest touch made her shiver with need.

She shuddered. "Galan?"

"I'm going to make you scream, my beauty. And then I'm going to eat you up."

She gulped at his darkly erotic words even as she shivered again.

He used one finger, sliding it back within her sheath using his thumb to gently massage the nub he found between her legs. "But first, I'm going to make you hot. And ready for me."

"I'm ready now." Her thready words were lost amid his chuckles.

"Not nearly enough." He withdrew from within her, slowly caressing the entrance to her core. "Feel what I'm doing to you. Close your eyes and enjoy the sensation."

She lowered her eyelids. How could she ignore his sensual demand? Her body was a rioting mass of excited nerves. She gulped, glorying in the sensation of caressing her way down his body. She captured him in her hand and stroked the tip of his cock. He jerked in reaction, rewarding Jessa with a long hiss.

Oh yes. Two could play this game. The thought quickly fled as he renewed his onslaught, tweaking her nipple while small explosions continued all the way through her.

"Oh God!"

He dragged her down to him, his kiss rapacious. He continued the sensual torture and she bowed away as he settled his mouth to her neck, finding the most sensitive point as she cried out.

"More." Her gentle demand urged him on.

Galan moved his fingers over her engorged flesh each time she leaned into his strokes, needing the touch of them inside her. But instead he teased, slipping around her core but not giving in to her request. She pumped him firmly feeling him jerk under her touch. Her breath came in urgent pants.

"Galan!" Her weak demand joined with a thrust and she rode the fingers she'd impaled herself on, needing the release.

With a grunt he pulled her up with him, then pushed her against the wall. She cried out at the loss of his touch but instead putting his fingers back where she needed them he gripped her hips. Lifted her and she wound her legs around him.

A single hard plunge embedded him deeply within her and she screamed at the exquisite pleasure, hanging onto his shoulders, lost in the maelstrom of passion. She arched while he advanced slowly but with intent. She rode him, took everything he had to give. The hairs at the juncture of his thighs abraded her where they rubbed against her sensitive flesh. Each movement intensified while her nipples made contact with his chest, the coolness of the wall against her hot skin and the slap of wet flesh added a dimension.

Her cries were broken, unable to form a coherent thought as her body sought the release it needed. The climax built with each slip of skin against skin, as Galan moved quickly, but before she could find the peak he would stop. "Not yet." His ragged words flayed her senses.

Then he would start again. Her heart pounded to the rhythm of their movements and her fingers lost their weak grip. "I can't..."

"More. More of you..." He panted the words and again she tightened her legs around him, squeezing him closer—her body screaming for the cataclysmic release.

Finally, he pumped one last time and her beleaguered senses shattered. "*Galan!*" Her scream urged him on. He battered at her, pumping harder and faster, no trace of the graceful man remained, just the primal lover demanding his pleasure, until he too held still against her. His seed jetting deeply within her and she leaned weakly against him. They slipped to the floor, the water still spraying over them.

GALAN CARRIED her to the bed. Her eyes closed and her body almost boneless. He smiled. This was something he looked forward to getting used to. Even as the thought came he knew he should hurry. The coolness of the room, probably from their temperature control system, chilled his body slightly and he shivered. Their damp skin would chill if he didn't get her under covers or dried off. Drying off would take energy and he was flagging. He'd never before experienced anything like the interludes he enjoyed with Jessa. Not only the strength of their lovemaking, but the constant need for it.

The *Quickening* certainly heightened their sensations, but it was more than that. He was sure of it. Was it love? He didn't know. He would have said he loved Gospah, but it was a faded sensation beside the emotions he experienced with Jessa. He wanted to remonstrate with himself. *Gospah had been a good and loyal wife.* But honesty was something he prized above all. His emotions had never been as fully engaged as they were now. He needed time to sort out the jumble in his head. If it was truly love, he needed time to woo Jessa before making any declaration; to make sure she felt the same level of bonding he did. To experience the intensity that shook him to the core. He knew she was not immune to his charms. He'd just seen that. He chuckled quietly. Yes he had most definitely seen and experienced that.

Even now his heart thudded in his chest and his mind still whirled in the aftermath. He laid her gently down, pulling the pale blue coverlet aside enough to make room for the two of them on the pristine white sheets and crawled beside her. He stared at the ceiling as thoughts chased around in his head.

"Ga'lan?" Her sleepy query made him smile. She didn't even seem to have the energy to look at him.

"Who else would it be?"

She snickered softly, but kept her eyes closed. "Don't care. Just want you. Forever."

His heart stuttered. He pulled the covers up and leaned over to kiss her gently on the lips. His body warmed a little and he sighed. The intensity of their lovemaking had him wrung out and even though a spark of arousal remained, his mind might be willing but his body couldn't react. Not yet. Perhaps with a little sleep. He laughed softly.

"Love you Galan." He heard the words.

He froze.

They startled him from sleep momentarily. *Can she mean it? Did she love him? Is it even possible?*

His brain tried to compute, but the exhaustion pulled at him, dragging him to sleep even as his mind wanted to make sense of the words.

Chapter 9

Jessa woke slowly. Sunlight spilled into the room and she snuggled closer, feeling a warm body. *Galan.* She smiled. Sometime during the night he'd slung one of his legs over hers and wormed one of his arms between her breasts, the slight weight both comforting and arousing. Her hair moved slowly with each exhalation. Her stomach rumbled and she remembered the love making session that had interrupted their planned dinner. It rumbled again and she moved, hoping not to wake him as she did.

"It isn't bothering me." His softly amused words surprised her.

"You're awake?" She turned in his embrace to be met with the touch of his lips firmly pushed against hers. The flare of heat took her and knotted her up inside once more. Just as it always seemed to do.

"Good morning to you too." She heard the amusement in his voice and cringed slightly realizing she hadn't even said the words.

"Good morning, Galan. How long have you been awake?"

He smiled broadly. "Long enough to know that you need feeding." But he moved his hand to pull her against him. He moved the other hand over her bottom, clutching it then kneading slightly.

She could feel his morning erection and shivered in delight.

"Now? Or should we order first?" She heard his sigh of regret as he pulled away. Surely they would have time and she grinned at the thought before rising and making her way quickly to the lounge area. Their clothes lay in piles strewn over the room and she picked them up as she went. It wouldn't do for housekeeping to find the remnants of their amorous activities.

On the desk sat the discarded folder with the room service menu, just where it had been left. She blushed hotly at the memory of their use of the desk last night. She gripped the menu in one hand and scurried back to the bed. "Here, if we order now, we might have time before we have to meet with the Prime Minister for some…fun."

He barked a laugh and the sensation of being wanted and whole filled her. *Desired.* He desired her.

"I like the way you think, Jessa." He grabbed the folder and opened it before thrusting it back to her. "Maybe you should order though."

She squinted at him. "Why?"

"I can't read it."

The instant he said the words reality intruded. *Of course he couldn't. No more than she could read his writing.*

"But if you can't read it, how did you manage to decode our language?"

"We used a decoder. It did a better than adequate job. However, I don't presently have one."

Galan's answer had her goggling. She wouldn't make a big thing of it, she decided. She would just have to learn his writing and he would have to learn hers. And their children would have to learn both.

Her heart stopped in her chest. *Children. Our children.* She gulped and pushed the thought aside. She couldn't afford to think like that. *Not now. Not yet. Nothing is settled.* But it was there, a vision of blonde children with berry colored skin in her arms. An ache settled in the region of her heart and for a moment dizziness engulfed her. Then she forced herself to return to reality, to remain calm. In silence she opened the folio and looked at the options. "A full breakfast or something light?"

He must have heard the tension in her voice as he raised an eyebrow. But he didn't ask and she was thankful. She wasn't ready to face the emotions that came with the vision yet.

"Whatever suits you." The words rumbled through the air. Reaching for the phone, she dialed in the order.

As Jessa hung up she swiveled. He lay back against the pillows, arms behind his head. Her breath caught. How on earth had she had the opportunity to not just meet this man but to fall in love with him? In the back of her mind sat another thought. *What if... What if I'm already pregnant with this man's child?*

Jessa stood quickly and backed away from the bed. "You know what? Maybe I should go shower and then dress. The food should be here soon anyway."

Then she fled the room and pulled the door on the bathroom shut behind her. Jessa clapped a hand over her mouth while she clutched her flat stomach with the other. *Oh God. What if I am?* Tears leaked from her eyes as she considered it. She hadn't been sexually active since Jace. Hadn't worried about any form of contraception and she was willing to bet he didn't either, given the situation on his planet. She moaned. A knock on the door roused her from the thoughts.

"Jessa? Jessa are you okay?" He sounded worried.

She couldn't blame anyone but herself. "Yeah... yeah I just..." She closed her eyes and made a decision. Opening the door she peered into his eyes. "What if I'm pregnant?"

He smiled. "Then that is indeed a miracle. But how would you know?" He reached for her face and stroked it gently as she laid her hand over his.

"I don't. But... What if I am?"

"Then we celebrate." But as if he understood her disquiet he pulled her gently into his arms. "It is that simple, Jessa. The *Quickening* and a pregnancy would seal it for me."

She swallowed the lump of anger and loss that lodged in her

throat. *Okay, so he doesn't love me, but will keep me because of some bond and a baby. Great work, Jessa.*

The ding of a bell filled the air and Jessa pulled away, thankful for the distraction. "Stay here. I'll get it." She grabbed one of the robes hanging on the bathroom door. Then she thrust her arms through the sleeves before belting it firmly and pushed past him.

THE MORNING HAD PASSED QUICKLY with the Prime Minister summoning Galan to her rooms. He wasn't sure he liked being called up like a servant. But he had to remind himself that it was necessary to go along with the fiction that he was just a captain. He could reveal his identity later—once an agreement had been forged.

She'd hurried them along organizing for them to travel to the location she kept calling the U.N. He was still unclear what it was. He remained amazed that there was no one central governing body for Earth, yet everyone kept telling him that this was the only way a decision could be made.

Jessa, meanwhile had been both cool and remote. He couldn't work out what was going through her mind but had his own issues to contemplate right now. He needed to formulate his argument before he spoke to what they called the General Assembly. Even that title confused him. Seth had tried to explain that it was an assembly of eminent beings and heads of state who came together to make decisions for and on behalf of the peoples of the many nations that made up their planet. To his mind, it seemed more senatorial and yet it didn't really have the same ability to legislate or bind them to the decisions taken.

On their arrival at the building he watched as people scurried here and there and huddled in small groups, sometimes pointing to him and turning back to whisper among themselves. He sighed, unsure if this was auspicious or not. Jessa sat next to him, her foot tapping and only participating when directly questioned. It was most unlike her, a situation which bothered him.

"Captain Galan? Could you come this way? The General

Assembly is ready for you now." He stood and extended a hand to Jessa. "No Sir. By yourself." The woman in the nondescript gray suit looked at him.

Jessa opened her mouth, but he shook his head. This time he would deal with this. She subsided but he saw how her lips pulled tight and she balled her fists. One of these days, she would surely explode, he allowed.

"No. Jessa, Seth and Joras come with me." He stated the words clearly, and watched as the woman frowned.

"One moment please." Then she scurried away beyond the door of the meeting room. He waited. Tense silence reigned.

She returned and smiled. "Of course. This way please." She indicated for him to follow and he did. Jessa walked beside him, his equal in so many ways, yet everyone kept throwing up obstacles, reminding her of her past and their view that she was somehow a lesser person. This couldn't be easy for her. His heart ached, aware she was out of her depth. He was about to begin negotiations for the future of his planet. The efficacy of his actions would affect those that would one day be his subjects. His own personal wants and desires had to take a backward step. After all, he could already see his own future in Jessa's eyes. That thought alone buoyed him.

The woman opened the doors and he could see the meeting chamber. Rows and rows of staggered seating, a large metallic panel loomed on the wall ahead of him, richly decorated in gold with an insignia on it. Beside it were two large screens. They stepped through into the hall and the imposing doors shut with a thud behind them.

The assembly waited in silence as the four made their way down the center aisle. He could feel each and every eye on him. On Jessa as she clutched his hand and on Seth and Joras to the other side. What he would give to read their minds. But he needed to focus and concentrate now. One misstep would mean the end of his mission. He couldn't fail. The future of his planet was in the balance.

Galan reached the front and the one called the Secretary General met him, shook his hand, pumping it up and down. His mind picked out facets to focus on. The women sitting at one table eyeing him, another set of delegates with white flowing headpieces whose arms waved as they talked in quick snatches.

"Please, come this way." The short man led him up the steps to the lectern and his people, Jessa, Seth and Joras found seats behind him. The usher motioned him forward.

"Ladies and Gentlemen, Please come to order. We now recognize the presence of Captain Galan of the Hesparian Galactic Fleet." A burst of applause followed and he bowed deeply. Even as he did, he drew in a deep breath and prepared himself, searching for a spot on the wall, looking for the doors they had just entered, just as he always did.

"Ladies and Gentlemen. I thank you for your welcome..." He started, talking slowly and clearly addressing the people of what he thought would be their fears. The room was silent and he outlined the situation on Hesparia, the background of how it had come about. What his planet had to offer to the people of Earth. From time to time he sipped on the water as he showed them images that Seth and Joras had prepared. And the whole time he hoped it would be enough to sway them. At the end he stepped away from the lectern, mentally exhausted he turned to Jessa. She rose to take his hand and they headed for the exit.

JESSA'S NERVES jangled as they slowly made their way up the aisle. She was aware of the many gazes focused on them. Many of the women leaned together and whispered and some of the men stared openly.

Galan had talked to them, discussing the health improvements he could bring. The technological advances his planet was happy to share. He'd woven a view of the opportunities for trade and diplomacy between the two planets and how that could enhance their quality of life. Of the other species they already had interaction with. He'd spoken with deep passion of the history and the development of his own, mainly agrarian based world.

She'd listened to the stories of the women who'd died knowing they had no choice in the matter. He told of the hollow emptiness of the adults whose children wouldn't be conceived and those who experienced the loss of hope that came with the death of a child before birth. How it was caused by the genetic manipulations that had occurred generations before his own. He'd shared the story of his own wife, Gospah. And during his speech Jessa bled deep inside, understanding now that he still grieved for her. Despite his protestations, she knew that all he could offer her was a corner of his heart. The rest would belong to his long dead wife and to any children she bore him—if they actually got that far.

He'd finished with the admonition, that now First Contact had been made, others would surely come. Some with pacific diplomatic notions. Others looking to colonize and form empires. Those who would see the lack of technology and see an opportunity. He spoke of the benefits of a diplomatic alliance, a sharing of knowledge. Of safety in numbers.

Once out of the chamber she pulled away. She needed time to think over his early statements in the chamber. "Galan? I need to visit the rest room." She avoided his eyes but saw him nod.

Now that he'd finished, he was silent. Jessa glanced to the door of the bathroom then back and waited for Danni to step beside her. They crossed the foyer together in silence heading for the room that had been pointed out to them earlier. Once the door shut behind her she let out a moan. She felt a touch at her back and she turned. Danni's face had lost its impassive façade. Instead she saw understanding.

"I've mucked the whole thing up." She muttered the words as much to herself as to her guardian.

"Do you think so? I don't see him trying to go anywhere that you aren't."

Jessa didn't know how to respond. Female friends were something she didn't have many of. But she needed another perspective. And she knew Seth wasn't the person she could ask. Her parents weren't talking to her and that really left pretty much nobody else.

"No. You see, he's not sticking around for me. It's a case of I could give his father and him what they most desire. An heir. A child. But did you hear him, up there?"

Danni nodded slowly. "I heard him speak of his planet and the loss of his wife. One he was close to. But I..."

"He loved her. It was there in the tone of his voice. She was everything a wife should be. Cultured. Capable. Artistic even." She repeated his words from the speech. "And they both wanted children. Something she couldn't give him." She turned away, her eyes burning once more.

"Jessa, I think you are selling yourself short. I mean... Do you even see the way he looks at you? The look on his face when customs wasn't going to let you into the United States?" Danni leaned forward, emphasizing her words. "He was ready to pull the plug on all this. For you."

But Jessa shook her head. "No." She couldn't believe that. Danni was seeing the incident with rose colored glasses. She'd seen the looks she and Seth were passing back and forth.

Seth was seriously smitten and she knew Danni was in the same boat. She had known lots of girls who, when presented with a male they were seriously interested in, only saw the same in others. It looked to her as if Danni were no different, in that department.

Instead she swallowed the frustration and pushed away from the door, making her way to the stall in the corner. She completed her personal business and when she emerged it was to see Danni watching her in the mirror, frowning, as she moved to the basin, washing her hands. "It's okay you know. It's better to know. That way I won't imagine he feels the same way..." She broke off.

"The same way you do?"

Danni's words pulled Jessa up short. *If Danni knows then how many others have worked it out?* "Don't tell him. He can't know." If he knew, he'd feel duty bound to respond. But it would be meaningless, because it would just be the words. She'd rather not open the subject than have him tell her something he didn't feel.

Danni's frown deepened. "It's not for me to do that, but Jessa... You need to tell him, at some point. If you are wrong..."

"No. I'm right. And it's better that he doesn't ever know. I don't want his pity. That's the last thing I want." Jessa hurried, pulling on a paper towel before she dried her hands. "We won't talk of this again." Danni nodded stiffly and she pulled the door open.

AFTER THEIR DISCUSSION in the ladies room, Danni and Jessa were careful to avoid any discussion of Jessa and Galan's situation. Jessa took an active interest in Seth and Danni's bourgeoning relationship. Unable to propel her own to a satisfactory conclusion, instead she helped Seth find every opportunity to sit beside and talk with Danni. A thrill of satisfaction filled her when on the fourth day Danni and Seth entered the suite, hand in hand, wordlessly telling Jessa what she'd hoped for.

Each morning Jessa and Galan woke in each other's arms and the nights were a passionate adventure. But the days were filled with endless rounds of meetings and concerns. Privately Jessa wondered if they, the delegates, were interested in stringing it out so they could enjoy the hustle and bustle of New York. Not that she had seen much beyond the walls of the United Nations building, the hotel and the vehicles they were shuttled in. By the fifth day she was wound so tight something was likely to blow. And she knew her own temper was frayed at the stress both she and Galan were struggling with.

Galan had woken early and organized their breakfast while Jessa showered and dressed.

"Jessa? We need to hurry. " His words filtered through the bathroom door. She grimaced before quickly covering it.

The delegates had no interest in anything she had to say. Indeed in her mind they had relegated her to the position of lover. Which, she silently agreed, was exactly what she was. She had no official standing beyond arm candy and even in that department she wasn't particularly useful. Even Seth had a role: He acted as an intermediary between Joras and the technical wunderkinds who had questions to ask about the various propulsion systems and technologies the Hesparians used.

But she, Jessa, couldn't even call on that. Feeling thoroughly sorry for herself she called back, "You know what? Why don't you go ahead I'll catch up later?" Silence reigned in the suite and she popped her head out of the doorway, scanning the bedroom as he wandered in.

"Are you ill?" His gaze, previously focused on her face dropped to her stomach. As if looking for some noticeable sign of pregnancy, her mind unhelpfully added.

"No. I'm not ill. But I just think, you are meeting with the Secretary General, the President and the British Prime Minister. You'll be busy. And I..." She cast about thinking for something to say. Any excuse instead of seeing that hopeful look in his eye. "I have stuff to do."

It was a weak excuse and shame filled her. Jessa released a sigh when he nodded in silence. She could tell he wasn't happy with her obviously badly executed argument but he didn't comment. He moved close, dropping a quick and almost cautious kiss on her lips. "I'll be back as soon as I can. If you come in, tell them..." He stopped and frowned. "Well, you know what to say."

Then he left. She heard the door open and close, behind him, she supposed. She stood still, holding herself rigid against the walls for an instant or two then slid to the floor. "God damn it Jessa. You are such a fool." Her eyes ached and she slumped. "He's more interested in whether you are pregnant than you. It's time to bail on this relationship." But it hurt. *God how it hurt.* She loved him. But it was an unequal situation. At least if he wasn't stuck with her around his neck, he might find another woman. One he loved. One who could compete with Gospah.

Once that decision was taken, she knew she needed to consider both the when and the how. Questions which turned in her mind even as her stomach cramped. When they went home, she would have to call it off. The answer was clear to her. Once they touched back down, she would thank him for the opportunity and walk away. He wouldn't be stuck with her and she could try to rebuild what remained of her shattered life.

She gathered herself up off the floor and headed to the bathroom. Her eyes were red and swollen from the crying jag. She grabbed the nearest facecloth. "Jessa, it may be nearly over, but you are not going to make him look foolish." She marched to the small refrigerator and grabbed a couple of ice cubes, which she wrapped in the thick white toweling and headed back to the bathroom.

She applied the impromptu cold packs and once she was satisfied that she had undone as much of the damage as she could she applied makeup. It was a little heavier than usual and she frowned at herself in the mirror. Then she hunted out her best clothes before scurrying into the living area where she grabbed her bag and keycard.

Opening the door to the corridor, she gazed at Danni, who'd pulled up a chair and waited. "Never thought you were coming out." Danni peered closely. "Are you okay?"

Jessa nodded, then she let loose a small laugh. "Of course I am." But Jessa was sure Danni could tell that inside she was falling apart.

They hurried into the elevator and when they emerged the manager scurried forward to escort them to the waiting car. As they strapped themselves in, Danni's phone rang.

"Hello?"

Jessa watched her eyes and saw them widen. Apprehension crawled over her body. What had happened? "They're ready?" The words were an excited squeak. "Okay... Yes, we're on our way."

As Danni hung up, Jessa urged her silently for information. "So? Who was that?"

"It was Seth." Jessa waited. "They are ready to make a formal announcement." Danni turned and rapped on the window. "Go as fast as you can."

The driver nodded, and made a quick call. Then the car shot forward.

GALAN PACED. He'd known something was wrong with Jessa and he couldn't understand what it was. He knew both Seth and Joras wondered what he was about. The last few days she had withdrawn, in subtle ways. But he was sure she understood that he had to resolve the situation with the people of earth. Then they could be together. And now, just moments ago, they had received a notification that a decision had been reached.

His skin crawled as if thousands of insects had invaded his clothes.

He reminded himself that he would focus on their relationship once this was out of the way. The days of to-ing and fro-ing had been endless. But his father had instructed him that any such meetings would be necessary to achieve the desired outcome. So he'd listened to their short sighted arguments. How would they pick the women? How could he guarantee their safety? He'd wanted to laugh in their faces at that. Safety? These women were in more danger of being smothered with affection by the men who desired life partners.

Then they had started trading for technologies, physician training and finally weaponry. He'd assured them that the technology was something the Hesparians were more than happy to supply and teach the humans to understand. The physician training could be handled by an exchange program. But the weaponry had caused him more than one concerned moment. They were a pacific culture, he had reminded them. Weaponry was something they had little interest in. After seeing the newscasts, he had already come to the conclusion that they might only use it to increase their territories. Something he knew his father would not entertain. So he'd put them off.

He'd also noted the way they'd eyed off Jessa. He'd been quite uncomfortable and angered with the dismissive way some people had treated her. But he'd kept his feelings on those matters to himself.

Lost in his own ruminations, he reacted with surprise as the door opened. Danni and Jessa entered together. He smiled. Not only would Jessa have Seth with her on Hesparia, but now she would also have Danni. He watched as the two women had forged a strong friendship. It pleased him that she would have a friend and confidante.

"Have they made the announcement yet?" Jessa asked the words in a rush. He gazed at her. She might be impulsive and impetuous, but she was also truly beautiful all the way through.

He reached for her hand. "Not yet."

She accepted his touch and that pleased him. He had a good feeling about today. After all, he had offered the people of earth a range of things that would've taken them generations on their own to achieve. And this morning's meetings had ended on what he would consider to be a positive note. He had made it clear they could not have their alliance without the agreement of the women migrating to Hesparia.

His people milled around, Joras waited silently on the seat reviewing notes and Seth and Danni sat together, their hands entwined. Seth would be invaluable to them when they got home to Hesparia. He would push for him to be absorbed into their Foreign Relations department. Danni could either take up a position in the same department or he could see if there was a suitable position for her in the guardian unit. He was sure that should the announcement go the way he envisaged it would be easier for all from this point on.

A knock came and he stood as the door opened. "Captain Galan? Could you and your people please join us in the Assembly Hall?" The young man who made the announcement indicated the room at the furthest point from where they had waited.

Galan nodded. The moment they had all been working for had come. They rose, and took positions, calmly traversing the corridor to the big doors which opened for them. They moved in silence down the steps toward the podium in the great hall. The Secretary General smiled in welcome and behind him the Prime Ministers of Australia, Great Britain and the President of the United States waited.

He could feel the trembling of Jessa's hand in his, but right now, he was focused on what was to come. His escorts indicated the position he had taken the first time he had addressed the assembly.

The Secretary General cleared his throat and opened with remarks about the enormity of the decisions they had been discussing. How they had never expected in their life to make any form of contact, let alone that it would be a diplomatic mission. Jessa squirmed slightly in her seat. Galan smiled, hoping that the talkfest would soon be over.

The Prime Minister of Australia then took over, telling about her first meeting and the things his people had already done for those in the small town where they had made their first contact. The healing that had occurred and the chance they could grasp to make leaps in health care. After she finished, she smiled almost benignly and Galan wanted to laugh at the attitude of motherly caring that sat so oddly on her face.

Then the Prime Minister of Great Britain took over. "We have taken every care to address the issues raised by members of the Assembly. In each and every meeting, we have carried your queries and questions to the Hesparian delegation." He stopped and scanned the assembly room. "We have taken your concerns on board and have sought ways to mitigate them."

"To that end…" The President of the United States took up the lead. "It has been resolved that we, the people of Earth enter into a diplomatic agreement with Hesparia. As an act of good faith, we give permission for three hundred women to migrate to Hesparia. They will be offered training, housing and if…" He stopped and Galan leaned closer, eagerly waiting the full pronouncement. "If they choose, they can then enter into a marriage-like agreement."

The speaker for Great Britain took over again. "We will also set up a diplomatic headquarters on Hesparia. Captain Galan has assured us that the requirements of transport will be made available to us and one will be placed in each of the continents of our planet. In return, Earth will enter into an exchange where our doctors and physicians learn from theirs and return home with that knowledge and skill. Technicians will travel to earth and train our best and brightest so that within seven years, we should have the capability and expertise to undertake interstellar travel on our own."

As the woman's words died away the room erupted into cheers and shouts. Not all positive he noted, but—he saw with satisfaction —the majority found the declaration to be positive.

"The process..." The American held up his hands, silently requesting the members to cease their noise and resume their seats, many having risen during the announcement. "The process of choosing the women will be undertaken by each country. Each of our member countries will be allotted a share of the positions."

Galan looked at Jessa, she was smiling but he detected a hint of sadness too.

"Why are you sad?" He spoke quietly to her, but she shook her head. This was a moment for triumph, not sadness. He wanted to grab her up but she looked away.

"Captain Galan?" The words surprised him and he looked up. "Will you address the assembly?"

He stood and made his way to the lectern, looking for some way to concentrate when he was both frustrated and concerned at Jessa's attitude. He looked out. The sea of expectant faces waited.

"On behalf of Hesparia. On behalf of my people, I thank you. And I thank your people." He inhaled deeply. "It is on this momentous occasion that we can take pride in the fact that our two races can once more be together. Learning to co-exist peacefully and enhancing each other's great civilizations. That together, united we can grow and develop safe in the knowledge that this is but the first of such diplomatic alliances that we shall form together." He bowed deeply and stepped away.

Jessa stood and smiled, but he could tell it wasn't a real one and his sense of disquiet grew again.

And in time to the beating of feet and clapping of hands, they followed the dignitaries up the stairs and out of the room.

THEY PROCEEDED TOGETHER to an office she had not previously entered and were invited to sit. Jessa took the seat furthest from Galan and the officials, checking out the heavy woods and reds of the décor. It was comfortably furnished but, to her mind, quite soulless. She much preferred Galan's office on the Princess Gospah and the way the ship reacted to her emotions.

She watched the dignitaries smile socially while refreshments were offered and she accepted a cup of tea. Galan had, during his time on earth, professed that he had enjoyed the taste of coffee so he accepted his and sipped. She drank in his mannerisms knowing their time together was coming to an end and trying hard not to let it show how deeply that knowledge cut.

The Prime Minister of Australia sat down opposite him. "So, let's nut out how many each country should provide to reach your target. I'd like to know just how you intend to transport them, of course." She smiled once more but as always, it never reached her eyes.

Galan inclined his head. "Of course. I have a ship waiting just beyond your moon. It has berthing facilities for six hundred, but with its crew of nearly ninety I feel that we can make the situation adequately comfortable on the six week journey."

The Prime Minister looked shocked. "You were so sure of our determinations?"

"No. But we wanted to be prepared in case you gave agreement. We will transfer them over a period of about a week in your time. My ship is capable of interplanetary travel, unlike the one awaiting us in Australia."

He smiled blandly. "Of course, we will send Seth and Jessa on the main ship to facilitate the comfort of the women."

"Oh dear. You do seem to be under some misapprehension. Neither should have an automatic entry into the ballot for migration." The President perched in his chair. "You see, with Miss Bankia's history and Mr. Bock's skills, neither would be what we would consider appropriate."

Galan tensed and Jessa watched nervously. "And you seem to be under some misapprehension, Miss Bankia and Mr. Bock have both become members of my crew in the last few weeks. They are upstanding and honest as well as loyal. I will not leave either behind." His face was set and his lips thinned. Jessa gulped as her stomach churned. She was not going to buy into this argument, because she knew she wasn't going with him.

"Captain Galan…"

He stretched forward smiling. "Actually in your terms, it's High Prince Galan. Jessa will be my consort. It is my intention that Seth will act as our technical advisor. I will not leave either behind." They sat back, their faces white with shock. Neither had seen his true position coming. As Jessa snuck a look, Agent Foley, Seth and Danni seemed to betray no surprise.

"I would also like to include both Agents Foley and McCall in advisory capacities for now. If you wish to draw from the three hundred to cover their inclusion, so be it." He spread his hands expansively.

They huddled together and Galan sat back, obviously very sure of himself and his position.

"High Prince Galan... We do feel, quite strongly that neither would be able—" The Prime Minister once more began only to be cut off, mid-sentence.

"Unless that is acceded to, then our agreement is over. Then you will need to propose to your world an alternative plan. This has already been announced. Amidst great fanfare. It will also leave our alliance in tatters. It's both or nothing." His eyes glinted and she saw their reactions to his comments and the air of determination. "Is it really worth the angst and embarrassment?" He smiled, easing back in his chair and Jessa was reminded of a crocodile. He looked to be all gnashing teeth and shining eyes, and she knew instinctively he was ready to argue with them. It was a side of Galan she had never seen before and she nearly shivered in reaction.

They huddled again for a moment, chattering urgently and there was shaking of heads, more quick talk followed by nods. The President now became their spokesperson. "Of course, we would be more than pleased to accede to your requests. How soon do you intend to begin the recruitment?" He was smooth, Jessa would give him that, watching as he switched gears from the vanquished diplomat to conciliatory conspirator.

Then they settled back, discussing the logistics of the ballot. Australia, England and America would each take fifty positions, leaving the remainder for other countries, allowing for those who conscientiously objected during the voting sessions. It would be based on a suitability matrix drawn up of those with the necessary abilities for an agrarian lifestyle, allowing for women between the ages of twenty one to thirty.

The meeting drew to a close and they left once more in the motorcade for the hotel, Galan and Joras both smiling widely. While Jessa brooded over what had taken place.

Chapter 10

Galan watched as Jessa lowered herself into the seat. After nearly two and a half...*weeks*—and he privately doubted he would ever get used to the human terms—in New York, he was ready to get back to the *Princess Gospah*.

They had finally signed the agreement just that morning, now that the ground rules had been fully agreed to. He reflected on the stiff formality of the signing. Jessa had attended and the lunch after, but her mood hadn't appreciably improved. In fact, if anything she'd become quieter and paler in the last week alone.

He sighed, picking up the sheaf of paper dictating the rules for the ballot. They had been circulated widely and applications were due to be received within the week. The flow chart were detailed and he checked them through, shaking his head at the paperwork each government had formulated to ensure what they considered to be an adequate process. Each application would be checked for suitability and the credentials of each candidate scrutinized. Then a ballot would take place in each location and the list sent to himself and Jessa for perusal.

It seemed a terribly long winded process to Galan, but he was happy to finally be able to have a date for the beginning of transportation of each of the women. Every prospective migrant had to be ready to travel within a week of the announcement of successful placement, flying into Sydney then shuttled via bus over to Parkes where they would be taken to the Princess Gospah.

He glanced at Jessa who had begun making lists of necessary items each woman would able to carry with her. Under her responsibility came weight restrictions, medicals and placement aboard the ship. Each woman would share a cabin with three others, hopefully encouraging them to interact and form lifelong friendships.

Jessa had rolled her eyes at the idea of all those women together in confined spaces for six weeks and mentioned that it wouldn't hurt to have a human female placed with them who ranked above them all. As a result, it was decided that Danni and Seth would travel with them on the mothership, now that they had declared themselves to be in a relationship, and Jessa would remain in constant contact with Danni.

But it still didn't ease his concerns over her behavior. "Jessa?"

She turned slowly, her eyes looking bruised and her skin pale. "Yes, Galan?" Her voice was thready.

He moved next to her, dropping to a crouch.

"You are unwell. When we get back to the *Princess Gospah* the healers will look at you."

She nodded tiredly. "I'm really exhausted, Galan. Do you think…?"

"Yes. Sleep will help." She inclined the seat and he found a blanket, draping it over her as she closed her eyes. He was worried about her. In his mind, he ran through her symptoms, ready to note them for the healers: Sleepiness, and even a touch of nausea now. Plus her body was so sensitive…

Sensitive breasts… Could she be…? He almost wasn't game to continue the thought.

He'd lost Gospah in childbirth. If Jessa was pregnant, then he would take extra special care of her. No way did he intend to lose the one he loved most.

Even as the thought crossed his mind his knees shook. *A child… The first in many years born on my planet.* Joy filled him, but he strove for a calm demeanor. He had never intended to let her go, but now, there would be no argument. In his mind, he started preparations. She would need to have her own things around her. That would mean taking her to her parents and brother to collect her belongings. He understood her relationship had become more than strained since they had become aware of his mission and her connection to him.

He sat down with his message cube and started listing what could be done to ease her workload. If she was pregnant then he would not allow her to overtax herself. As he watched the clouds passing by the window and she continued to sleep, he found himself looking at her, taking in her pale countenance again and again and he knew and accepted the truth: He loved her. He smiled.

JESSA WOKE as the plane landed. She didn't feel refreshed. Her stomach churned and she was sure she was about to be sick everywhere. She slipped a hand over her mouth and one over her stomach as it lurched uncertainly.

She must have made some sound because Galan was there. "Here, let me help you." He had her on her feet and cleared the way to the bathroom where she was violently ill. She was sure she was about to die as her stomach roiled and jostled.

After several minutes, breathing carefully through the worst of it, the feeling passed and she rose unsteadily to her feet. Galan was there again, offering her a damp cloth to wipe her face and a glass of water to wash the taste of bile from her mouth. The most overwhelming emotion that flooded her was embarrassment. How could she throw up on him like this? Jessa raised a shaking hand to her clammy forehead feeling increasingly foolish. "Galan... I..."

He folded his arms around her. She wanted to cry as her knees wobbled.

"It's okay Jessa. Let's get to the vehicle and get you settled."

From that point on he treated her like spun glass. Collected her bag and coat then helped her down the steps to the waiting car.

Once settled in the air conditioned comfort she began to feel a little better. A bottle of water was pressed into her hand and a packet of dry biscuits.

"Try these. They should ease your stomach." He slipped into the vehicle beside her and tugged her against him. Feeling so weak and useless was something she had little experience of, and it wasn't a comfortable emotion, she decided wearily.

It's probably some twenty four hour bug I've picked up in New York. As they travelled the kilometers back to Parkes, her body resumed its usual rhythm once again. But Galan was acting edgy. When they stopped he'd almost escorted her all the way to the ladies and made Danni stand outside the door of the stall. Jessa decided that even though she understood his fears it was overkill. And something she would discuss with him later. Then the realization hit. There would be no *later*, for them. She swallowed the sense of loss that clawed at her and smiled. Once they were back in the car, he cuddled her close against him. He had been affectionate before, but now he seemed to be making some kind of personal statement. She wasn't entirely sure what it was, not that she really had the energy to even try to decode it.

By the end of the third hour, somewhere past Orange she was settled enough to fall into an uneasy sleep.

This time she dreamed and it was a jumbled and upsetting mix of images. She was leaving. Galan watched as he made to step onto the eli-pad but he turned one last time, to bid her farewell and she could see something in his arms. Something wrapped in a blanket, which he held close against his chest. She woke realizing that silent tears dripped down her cheeks.

"Jessa? My love, do not cry." He slid a gentle hand through her hair. His touch so gentle it almost broke her heart again. She looked out the window to see the town of Parkes ahead. The time to say goodbye was almost here and heaven help her, she wasn't sure she was strong enough to do that.

They pulled into the road that would take them to the dish installation and to the *Princess Gospah*. She saw that the number of protestors had increased. Vehicles blocked the entrance and at the sight of them they chanted and shouted. Eggs and rotten tomatoes were thrown at the car and the placards waved at them.

Police formed human barriers allowing them to pass and she trembled. What would her life be like once she returned to reality? Would they picket where she was? Of course, she could take the easy way out. Stay with Galan and go to Hesparia. The option was there, and honestly, it was tempting. But she wasn't a fool. He didn't love her. He wanted her because of the bond formed by the Quickening and any chance of a child. It wasn't enough though. She needed him to love her and want her for her. And if that wasn't there, she wouldn't grovel for whatever scraps of affection might come her way. *I have far too much dignity to settle for that*, she told herself firmly.

Silent tears trickled down her face, scorching her cold skin. She quickly dashed them away with unsteady hands, hoping he wouldn't see them.

Jessa remonstrated with herself internally. She would complete the tasks she had taken on, preparing the lists of migrants for Hesparia, organize the berths. She'd had weeks to prepare herself for this. Once on board the *Princess Gospah* she would tell him.

They turned in, finally past the protestors and the vehicle stopped right beside the ship. She waited patiently as he told her to stay in the car. His people swarmed, collecting the baggage and carrying it to the *Princess Gospah*. Then with a tender smile he held out his hand for her. Feeling even more like a fraud, she accepted it and followed him to the eli-pad.

IF GALAN WASN'T MISTAKEN, Jessa had something on her mind. And it wasn't pleasant. But whatever it was, he'd bet it could be fixed soon enough. She followed him into his cabin and sat down on the bed, her face downcast. A knot formed in his belly.

"Galan… We really should talk."

The undertone chilled him. He moved to the bed beside her. "What about?"

She sucked in a deep breath and he knew. Somehow his mind told him she was planning to leave. Without him.

"About us. This." Her hand waved at the room. "Our situation… It's not healthy for either of us."

He formed fists with his hands. "I'm not sure why you'd even think that…" He was about to launch into all the reasons they were good together. The most important of them, being that he loved her. But he couldn't tell her of the revelation that he'd had watching her on the plane as she slept. He didn't think she was ready for that. Not yet. He didn't want her to think he only wanted her for the child.

"I can't stay, Galan. It isn't right. I know you told them all that I was going to be your consort… But I can't be." She turned away, covering her face with her hands. A sob erupted and her shoulders shook as he watched.

Chilled to the center of his bones.

She didn't love him. She wasn't going to stay with him.

His heart shattered.

But he couldn't give her up. Not without at least trying, so he placed a hand on her shoulder. "Jessa… I don't…" He sucked air into his lungs. "I can't let you go." The strangled words hung in the air. He wouldn't take them back, even if he wanted to. It was true. *I can't let her go.*

"Galan…"

He pulled her back against him and she was still in his arms.

"Don't make this harder." Jessa turned and her eyes were pools of agony. "What we had was always going to be transitory. We never made any promises to each other. We never said we loved each other…" Her voice broke on the last words and he clutched her tighter.

Her words made him flinch. He wasn't going to lose her. Not like this. If it meant pushing her, then he would damn his own ethics and morals. "Maybe I didn't… but I do." At his words, Jessa pulled away.

"Don't patronize me!" She spat the words at him, anger warring with her pain.

"I'm not! I've loved you from the first time I saw you."

She stopped dead. Her face lost every touch of angry color so that only a pale visage remained. For an instant he thought she might faint.

Then she squared her shoulders. "You do not. You're just saying the words to humor me. Fine, I might love you, but don't cheapen it. Don't ever cheapen my feelings!" She shouted and warmth flowed through him. The first since the conversation began and he wanted to shout his joy.

She loves me! Hot on that realization came the thought that she didn't believe him. *How can I…?* Even as he caught the thought, the answer was clear. "Wait! Just one moment. Be quiet and listen to me."

Tear tracks glistened on her cheeks and his heart thudded. "I'll prove it to you. Just give me a minute." He scrubbed a shaking hand over his face. It was the most important thing he'd ever have to prove. "Gospah?" He called on the ship. The lights dimmed and the walls pulsed.

"Galan? Jessa? How can I be of service?" The tone was cautious. She'd been listening.

"Gospah? Tell Jessa what I am feeling."

Jessa looked at him startled.

"Galan? I don't usually…" The words were hesitant but he smiled.

"Go ahead. This is one time where your intervention in private matters is appreciated."

"Galan feels happy, just as he always is, with you. When you came onboard he was concerned. When you told him you were leaving the aura was dejected. Once you told him you loved him, it lightened and warmed. Given the array of feelings, I deduce that he's a man in love—in love with you, Jessa."

She sat still, holding onto her arms tightly as if holding in the emotions. He waited patiently she scanned his face. "You can't…" A single tear drop shook on her lashes. Then it released and slipped down her face. The emotions left his heart clenching. "You… " She stopped, placed a shaking hand over her lips. "You love me?"

He nodded. Waiting for her to see the truth. The one he had not long realized himself.

With a single sob, she threw herself into his embrace. "I love you too. But I thought… I thought it was the chance at a baby…"

He growled. "A baby with you would be the thing that would complete us. But what I want is so much more. I didn't know really until the plane… But to spend my life time with you? To have you at my side as my consort is the one thing I want. The thing I need to fulfil me." He pulled her into his arms. "I want forever with you Jessa. Because I love you. You for you, not for what you can give me or my people. So if that thought is still there, banish it now."

She wound her arms around him and he pulled away to slip a careful finger under her chin, lifting her mouth to his. Then he kissed her.

JESSA PULLED BACK AND SHIVERED. After all her concerns and mistaken belief, now she knew the truth—that he loved her. *So close.* She'd come so close to throwing it all away because she thought she knew best. The thought nearly overcame her and her stomach clenched slightly before she allowed herself to savor her new found knowledge. Now here they were, on his bed. *In his cabin.* Together.

She wanted him. An ache started in her heart and travelled all the way down to her core.

"Gospah?" She waited and the walls pulsed in deep shades.

"Yes Jessa?" She smiled as the subdued tones of the ship.

"Could you … umm…" She giggled. The thoughts that now echoed in her head were fairly lascivious. She certainly didn't want Gospah there for the scenes she was about to enact with Galan. That is, if he was of the same mindset. She glanced at him and saw the growing understanding.

"Of course, Jessa. Excuse me, please, Galan." The amused tone died away and the walls glowed a dull red, letting them both know that she had withdrawn.

"Now then… Let me see… Where were we?" She slipped her

hands around Galan's waist. "Oh yes..." She leaned in and almost at his lips, whispered, "right about here." And pressed herself to him. She placed her mouth against his, which opened and she thrust her tongue within the warm moist cavern.

She firmed her hands over his shoulders, glorying in the feel of him beneath her touch. His hands shook as he circled her waist. He gripped her with hard fingers. "Let me love you." He whispered against her lips and the breath caressed the sensitive skin. His words became a drug, pulling at her senses and she closed her eyes just a little until her lids were at half-mast.

Slowly he brushed one hand up her side, letting it settle beside the swell of her breast. Then he followed slowly with the other and she quivered beneath his careful movements. If only he knew exactly what each caress and glance did to her. How she burnt when he was near.

Jessa kept her fingers on his collar bone but slid them in slow circles and he moved into her touch, as if seeking more. "You are the most beautiful woman I know." Galan brushed his thumbs up and down the sides of her breasts and she shivered in reaction. Hot sparks of arousal exploded within her body.

His touch moved, sliding across her breasts and she cried out. He stopped and looked into her eyes, his concern clear. "Okay?"

"Just a bit sensitive at the moment." She gasped the words.

He smiled warming her through at the gleam that entered his eyes. "And I've barely begun." Gently, he lowered his head again. This time the kiss was like the brush of a butterfly's wing, so very soft and tender.

She made to open her mouth but he pulled back. "Not yet." He gently nipped his way down to her chin and nibbled, then continued the sensual journey up to the sensitive spot beneath one ear. "Tonight, I'm going to love you like no one ever has or ever will again."

He flicked his tongue against tender flesh and she shivered in delight. "Galan, please." She raised her hands to lock around his neck but he caught them, stilled them. Raised them above her head.

"Not tonight, Jessa. Tonight is the first night of our forever." The meaning of his words made her teary.

"Oh Galan… I nearly made the biggest mistake of my life. I…" He stopped her words with another soft kiss.

"But you didn't." Galan placed his hands on the front of her blouse, buttons popped slowly and she watched his movements. Finally he pushed the material away, exposing the white bra that lay beneath. "So very beautiful."

He traced the top band of her underwear and her breath hitched. She squirmed again, knew that at this rate, she'd explode before he even entered her. "Galan…" Her breathless entreaty was met with a seductive and low chuckle.

"Be patient." He reached behind, deftly unfastened her bra and she hissed as the cool air caressed her sensitized globes. This time he groaned and placed his hands over her. Flicked the distended nubs he found and she jerked in response as lightening flashed through her system.

He had barely touched her and already her body was over-stimulated. She pushed against his chest. "My turn." But he stopped her, shaking his head.

"No. Tonight is for us, but I need to show you how much I care." His face was tight and hard like granite and his eyes glittered with need.

Jessa subsided and let him continue his intimate inspection. But each touch heated her system. Her core yearned with emptiness and she moaned as he moved his hands to the waistband of her pants.

He tugged at them and she rolled her hips, letting him push them down her legs. She sat on the bed, in just her panties as she squeezed her knees together while excitement gripped tight. "Galan!" She called his name and this time he crooned to her.

"Jessa. Sweet beautiful Jessa. My heart and my love." He brushed his fingers over her mound, hidden beneath the plain white cotton and she moved mindlessly. Slipping one finger beneath, parting the damp curls, he dipped within her. She arched and panted.

"More Galan. I need more!" Her broken cries mixed with the

Galan smiled. "Think, Jessa. You are ill, you complain of sore breasts. You tire quickly. They are all symptoms."

Jessa gasped as he enumerated those that had occurred to her. "Pregnant? You think I'm pregnant?"

He nodded.

She gulped. If that was true, this would be the first child on Hesparia in many years.

"If you wish, we can ascertain if that is indeed what is making you ill." His quiet words soothed the last of her fears. He helped her stand.

She needed to know. "How soon can we find out?" Now she wanted to know. Yearned to find out if she was carrying his child.

"We can find out immediately. I will send for one of the healers." He kissed her cheek and helped Jessa back to the bed. She lay down, still wrung out from exertion but filled with excitement. *Could it really be true? Could she be lucky enough to have Galan and a baby?*

"Gospah? Could you request one of the healers to come to my cabin? He will require his diagnostic equipment." He sat beside Jessa, the bed dipping slightly, rolling her towards him. He smiled and caressed her cheek.

"Of course, Galan. Should I give him details of the symptoms?" The walls flushed with pastel shades and Jessa nearly laughed, controlling the urge with some difficulty.

"Not at this time."

They waited, only leaving the bed to slip into light robes, then the door opened and one of the healers entered with the diagnostic tool in his hand. She couldn't remember his name but had met him during her time aboard.

"Galan, you required my services?"

Galan smiled broadly. A hot tide scorched her cheeks. *This was so embarrassing.* But now that the idea was there, she wanted to know. Needed to know and desperately wanted it to be true.

Galan explained her symptoms and Jessa waited patiently as the healer sampled her blood, then peered into the tiny screen. A small smile crept over his face. He turned the screen for Galan to view.

"So?" She demanded to know what the results indicated.

Galan smiled at her. "It's positive. We are going to have a child!" His eyes glowed with delight and warmth flowed through her. *A baby. Hers and Galan's.*

"Sir… Will you be wanting Jessa to be moved to the medical facility?"

Jessa was startled. Why on earth would she need that? Was there something wrong with her? With the baby? "Do I… Do I need that?" The happy and warm feelings dissipated. "I really don't want to spend the next months in some medical facility unless there is a reason." She leaned in, pinning the healer with a questioning gaze.

Galan put an arm around her. "It is a precaution we usually take because of the issues…" He turned to the healer. "Is it really necessary?"

The healer looked perplexed. "Honestly? I don't know." He shrugged his thin shoulders. "Jessa doesn't have the altered gene, so it may be unnecessary, but still… I'd like to keep a close eye on her, during the gestation period. Remember, we don't know the effect on the fetus either."

Galan had paled during the exchange and nodded slowly. "I had not considered that." He gripped her hand painfully. "Perhaps…"

But Jessa wasn't about to be sequestered for the next however long. "Look, I won't go to the medical facility, but I'm more than happy for you to keep a close eye on me." She hoped he would agree to her solution. "I'm not doing anything taxing. Organizing the migration of the women and their berths seems to be about my limit of tasks. I promise not to do anything strenuous and check in as regularly as you need. So, will you let me remain here, in the normal cabin?" She waited, hoping they would see that it was the wisest option.

Both the healer and Galan watched her for a moment then the healer nodded. "If you are unwell, ache, hurt, bleed or other, you must report to me immediately. Do you understand?"

Jessa nodded. This baby was far too precious to her, to Galan and to Hesparia for her to take any chances. "I will."

Obviously satisfied, the healer left the room.

Chapter 11

Jessa stretched. The table and chairs that had been made available for her use were comfortable but her pregnant body was disinclined to let her sit still for so long. She regularly needed frequent bathroom breaks. As the announcements of women who were to migrate to Hesparia came in, she needed to deal with all manner of requests. This one had an allergy to peanuts, that one absolutely had to have a bath. Another ate no pork on religious grounds. One couldn't part with her Elvis Presley memorabilia and wanted to ship it to Hesparia.

Mounds of paper sat at the end of the desk. Jessa groaned reading the requests. She called out when someone knocked on the door.

It opened and her assistant entered the room. "Jessa? Where do you want these?" The files in her hand bulged as did all the others littering her desk.

"Start a new pile, Emily. I'll get to them after I finish all the others." She indicated the rubble on her desk. "And Emily? How many more are due in?"

"Well, we have the first hundred now. Their references have been checked, they have already attended their mandatory medicals.

If you sign off on this list today, they should arrive in the next week. As soon as you okay it, I can arrange their flights into the air force base and then sort out their transportation to Parkes." Emily smiled and Jessa considered for an instant requesting her presence on board but shook her head. Emily had a young man she was seeing. It wouldn't be fair.

Trying to avoid the twinge of her bladder, Jessa sat back. "Okay then. I have arranged the first sixty berths, forming them into small groups as Galan suggested. That should make keeping track of them easier. He is going to have them transported to the cruiser on arrival, but I'd like to get the next lot organized well before they arrive." Jessa thought of the three weeks she had been ploughing through the details. Each woman's file had to be transmitted to them. After that had been trying to work out the best way to group the women and arranging details of the amount of luggage each was allowed to bring." She yawned again.

"Jessa, I don't like to pry… But, are you okay?" Emily peered at her and Jessa knew she had her suspicions. Ones that she and Galan had decided to ignore as best they could. They both agreed making any form of announcement could increase the probability of attack. So far, they had managed to ignore the constant protestors although their numbers had dwindled, but if word leaked out… *A human hybrid…* Well, they could well imagine the outcome. So instead, Jessa smiled. "I'm fine. Just caught a flu and still trying to shake off the after affects."

She could see Emily was unconvinced but there wasn't much else she could do. Instead she smiled brightly. "Leave those files here and I'll keep going."

Emily popped the files on a clear spot on the heavy wood desk.

"Oh look at the time. Galan will be sending the car soon. Let me know when it arrives." If she could end the conversation and get Emily out of there she could stand and use the small toilet at the back of her office.

Her assistant nodded and left the room. Jessa gave her a moment and stood, stretching her back before she headed for the bathroom.

As she returned, she heard a noise outside in the corridor. "Emily? Is everything okay?" She headed for the door, but sprang back as it crashed open.

Jace and a man she didn't recognize stood before her.

Jessa backed away. "How in hell did you get in here?" She narrowed her eyes, hoping to distract the two while she surreptitiously pressed the distress button below her desk.

"Jessa. You should have realized I was going to come back for you. After all, you were mine before and I don't want to see you sullied by that filthy alien." He advanced and while her senses screamed at her to retreat, she stayed firm. *Where in hell are Danni and Emily?* Her stomach jostled at the thought that something might have happened to them. Particularly Danni. She'd grown very close to the agent who was now Seth's lover. "Where are…?" Her voice broke a little and Jace smiled.

"Where are the two women?" She needed to know. If she'd thought he cared a whit about Seth, she would have revealed that Danni and Seth were very much together as a couple, but she feared Jace would only see that as leverage.

"The women?" He chuckled and the evil sound soured her stomach. "Unfortunately one tried to stop me. I had to take some steps… I had to stop her, a little more permanently than planned. The other? Well, I don't know if or when she'll be coming around."

Danni? Emily? Can they both be dead? Because Jace wants me for some misguided plan that will supposedly prove the strength of his cult? "Why on earth do you want me so badly?"

He stopped. "I didn't think you were so blind. But then… When I think back on the heist, I forget how trusting you can be."

The man with him snickered.

She backed away as they came closer.

"You have become very well known. In fact, you are the face of inter-species relations these days. That makes you a valuable commodity." He smiled as he indicated his friend should come closer.

Jessa backed up further, finding herself against the cold, hard wall. The man grabbed her wrist in a painfully tight grip.

"If I can get you to renounce the evil that the aliens represent, then we have a hope of stopping this purchase of human brides."

He squeezed her wrists in his meaty hand, winding a cord around them. The grip pinched and she cried out. "Now, now, Jessa. There's nothing to be a baby about. We just want to be sure that you stay with us." He leered.

Then she was shoved forward roughly. "We should tape her mouth up, so she can't cry out."

Jace nodded, reaching into the backpack she hadn't seen on his shoulder. He fished around and as Jessa opened her mouth to cry out the man holding her clapped a hand over it. Jace threw the tape to her captor who caught it in one hand. The first real stirrings of panic nearly drowned Jessa. She had to get out of this... Away from Jace, his henchman and this mad plot.

The rip of the tape caught her attention as he lifted his hand. She screamed loudly. He hit her, just a glancing blow but enough to make her head ache and stop the noise. Then the tape was shoved over her lips and mouth, stopping any further loud sounds from escaping. She tugged and pulled as he gripped her other arm and tied the two wrists together then the intruder laughed again.

"Now Jessa, I do apologize for Michael's behavior, but you must understand. It is necessary for us to stop you making decisions that will affect your life negatively." Jace ogled her and not for the first time she found her skin crawling as she thought of the one single night she had allowed him to touch her.

"Jace? We'd better be leaving." The man, Michael, indicated to the door and Jace nodded.

They both gripped her arms at the elbow, pulling her along to the doorway. She twisted and fought but neither of her assailants paid her much attention while they towed her along. As she got to the door, she stuck out a foot, trying valiantly to stop the motion. *Don't let them take you somewhere else,* ran like a recording in her head and she tried to hold on to the jamb, scraping her skin when they tugged her away.

She slipped and fell but they picked her up. With muttered

imprecations the big man swung her up, over his shoulder like a bag of potatoes.

Jessa kicked out. A grunt told her she'd hurt him so she did it again. This time he hit her with his palm across the head. It already ached and this made the situation worse. Things looked grim and she tried to focus on a way to escape.

GALAN SAT IN THE OFFICE, watching his chronogram, waiting to reach the time he could take Jessa home. His small palm unit held strategic information to help them reach Hesparia. He'd been calculating the levels of fuel required allowing for the extra passengers and weight allocations as well as preparing a report to transmit to his father. He had avoided this until he had some definite information to give him.

The buzz of the telephone caught his attention. *I much prefer communicators.* He lifted the antiquated receiver to his ear. "Galan here."

"Sir? Captain?" The voice on the other side had an uncertain and worried sound to it. It caught his attention immediately. "There's a situation. Miss Bankia's office panic button has been enabled."

Galan was out of his chair, his system flooding with adrenalin. He tapped his communicator. "Joras? Get the security team. Jessa's office has been breached." He castigated himself. After weeks of quiet they'd stopped expecting anything to happen and had relaxed their security protocols.

He stalked the distance between his office and door and wrenched it open. They'd been placed in two different buildings. And even though they were side by side, she had her own personal guard in Danni. What had happened to her? He didn't want to think about it. He knew Jessa was fond of the woman and he admitted to some level of affection for the woman who had paired up with Seth.

Joras met him at the door. "I have the men ready to go in.

But…" His friend looked at him and Galan knew his thoughts, having been taken into their confidence during the briefing session for this part of the mission. They didn't want to risk Jessa or the child with a mistake. His stomach clenched.

"We have to get her out safely." He growled as rage coursed through him. The intelligence that Agent Foley had shared was that Jace was under surveillance and unlikely to be a problem. But he had privately shared his disquiet with that analysis. Jace had been seen in the area lately. He knew which building they worked in, having been spied driving by and he'd previously considered his interest in Jessa was quite specific. But with no action, they had all believed he'd given up.

"Whatever it takes, Joras."

Joras put a hand on his arm and he had to fight to stop shrugging the comforting touch away. "We'll get her out safely."

Their men piled into the corridor, laser pistols in hand. With a single nod they moved, flowing against walls as they headed out to save the consort of their prince. Galan watched, a feeling of helplessness overcame him.

Jessa. His Jessa was in danger.

He leaned against the wall and closed his eyes as fear overtook him.

JESSA KICKED OUT AGAIN, this time earning an oomph. The man stumbled. She pushed against him in that instant and managed to break free of his hold. There was no way she was going to give in easily. With a thud, Jessa hit the floor and used her knees to shove herself away as quickly as she could. But it wasn't nearly quick enough as someone grabbed her ankle. She kicked out again, striking flesh and tried to scramble in the opposite direction. "Stay still bitch!" Jace grabbed her hair. With a single move he cracked her head against the floor. She lay, panting and moaning behind the tape. *Galan!* Her heart cried out to him, but this time she was sure all was lost.

Tears and wet sticky liquid seeped down her face, stinging her eyes while she lay on the floor. She spied a hand beneath the desk that was in her line of sight. It moved and twitched, feeling her stomach roil at the pain that racked her head. It waved slightly and she peered as hard as she could. A face. *Danni.*

Danni frowned at her, lips firming in anger. Jessa took heart and made to struggle again, but Danni shook her head while her mouth formed a 'no'. Jessa stopped. Understanding came in a wave. She was looking for an opportunity. Jessa blinked once to show she understood and stilled her shaking body.

"About time you came to your senses." *Jace.*

He gripped her shirt and pulled her upright, preparing to put her over his shoulder like a sack of potatoes again, no doubt. "Don't fight me, or you won't like the consequences. He purred the words as he slid his hand over her breast.

She recoiled.

He laughed. "Maybe you'll like it so much, you won't want to go back to him. After all, how well can an alien fuck anyway?" Her stomach heaved at his words and he must have heard the moan, her body clenched reacting to him. "Not going to be sick on me, are you?" His voice sounded uncertain and a shudder wracked her as he tried to heave her up.

In that instant, Danni sprang from her hiding spot with a long and heavy stapler in her hand. She charged. Michael stepped in front of Jace and they grappled. Michael might have size on his side, but Danni was trained and angry. She threw him with some kind of martial arts move and had him dropped to the floor, doubled over and sobbing as she sank the toe of her boot into his guts. Then she headed for Jace. He started running.

Jessa bounced on his shoulder, each move jarring her tender head. Danni jumped and caught him, flying in his direction and he moved with a jerk and a howl. He turned and Jessa could see the way he fished in the pocket of the light blue jacket for something. Danni stopped and swore. Jessa couldn't see why, slung against his back, but she started moving. Jessa kicked out at him while she twisted and turned in his grip.

Danni grabbed at him as the door at the back of the building crashed open.

Jace stopped dead in the middle of the hallway. "Fine. Anyone move and I'll kill her." With a single move, Jace hauled Jessa to the floor and pressed something cold and round into her side.

Dear God. Was it a gun? Sobbing with fright, Jessa stood motionless. How were they going to get out of this? She shuddered with fear and he hauled her closer. "Stay still, damn it."

She looked into his wild eyes, seeing how they scanned from side to side. What chance did she have? They wouldn't let Jace take her and he'd rather her dead than with them. She moaned again behind the tape. He looked down.

In that instant, Danni sprang again, throwing herself upon the arm that held the gun. A bang was met with a fzzt. Jace fell and so did Danni with a loud thud.

Jessa hit the floor with a stunning blow. This time was one injury too many and she passed out.

JESSA WOKE to find Galan looming over her. "She's waking up."

The sound of is voice was so darned loud. She winced. "Could you...you know, keep it down a little?" Her head hurt, her lips stung and itched and wherever she was lying on wasn't terribly comfortable.

Then it came rushing back. The attack when Jace had broken into her office. "Danni? Emily?"

Galan frowned.

"The baby?" He turned and she saw the healer who had seen her before.

His long thin face sported a deep frown as he checked her over. "The fetus seems to have weathered the attack infinitely better than Jessa." He shook his head. "I'd really prefer to have her back at the ship now."

Galan rose to his knees and Jessa realized she was lying on the carpet.

"She'll be fine to carry?" Galan looked at the healer who nodded slowly. With great care he lifted Jessa into his arms and pushed off the floor with a grunt. She winced a little as the action jarred her aching head and a buzzing sound rang through her brain.

"Danni?" Galan looked at her, obviously the thin sound of her voice concerning him.

"She'll be fine. She only received a flesh wound from the bullet and has a good size lump on her head."

She opened her mouth to ask about Emily and caught the look in his eye. "Emily didn't make it."

Jessa sighed even as her eyes ached. Emily shouldn't have died. There was no reason she should have been involved. She'd been in the wrong place at the wrong time. "Has someone...?"

"We will allow the police access once you and Danni have been safely removed." Galan's voice was short.

She let her head rest against his shoulders and kept her eyes closed. Muscles in her legs and arms ached. Her wrists ached and she rested weakly, drawing comfort from the feel of him holding her so tightly.

Galan barked out commands in his own language and she burrowed in, soaking up the warmth of his touch. Sounds of muted footsteps came from behind her and she looked around, the room spun crazily as her stomach flip flopped.

Agent Foley stood there, his face white. "Galan... Jessa..."

"She's safe for now and so is Danni. Unfortunately Emily is deceased. I'm taking Jessa back to the ship and Danni has already been sent on."

"I will personally escort you to the ship."

Jessa couldn't remember the man ever sounding so tense or on edge, but the ache in her head was finally subsiding. Galan carried her out the office and to the vehicle. He was careful but she was still jostled. She moaned as her uncertain stomach reminded her of her current state. Wincing a little at the loud sound of the door closing. He pulled her against him. The car rocked, and movement lulled her into a twilight state. Each time she almost dozed off, Galan would call her name.

The ride seemed interminable, the chants and jeers from beyond the car irritated her and she wanted to scream. *Can't they see this is what their people have done? Not hers. Hers were pacific. Only doing what had to be done to keep themselves safe.*

They pulled up next to the eli-pad and Galan carefully lifted her out. They climbed aboard. The ship was almost silent as they traversed the corridor. Galan finally arrived at their cabin, setting her down carefully.

"Now you are safe." She opened her eyes at his grim tone.

What did he mean by that? She wasn't sure she liked his tone at all. "What are you going to do Galan?" She could hear the peevish sound and didn't care.

"From now on, you will work from the ship. You will be protected at all times. I can't go through that again, so don't even bother asking."

She wanted to argue at his words, but heard the underlying fear beneath. Her head ached and she really didn't want a fight. She didn't think there was anything she could say that didn't sound like an agreement to his terms.

The healer entered the room and Galan stepped aside.

He held a small spray applicator against her neck and a cooling sensation followed. Her head began to settle and as a result her stomach did too. She made to rise but the healer held a hand flat against her shoulder.

"You must lie still for at least three hours while the medication takes effect. I can't give you anything stronger as we don't wish the babe to be harmed."

She moved her hand to cover her still flat belly. "It's…" She stopped and gulped as concern flooded her system. "It's okay, isn't it?"

"For now. But we must look after you and that child… All children are precious." He bowed deeply.

She saw how his face paled as he left. "Did he lose someone too?"

Galan nodded. "His wife and three babes."

She gulped, finally realizing just how much they had all been hurt by the results of the experiments. The planet must have drowned in tears. "Can I...?" She stopped.

Galan dropped to the bed beside her. "Tell me what you want and if it's in my power, I will do it." He whispered the words as he carefully moved the strands of hair from her face.

"I want to see my parents."

He frowned. "I won't take you to them." His voice firmed and she finally understood.

"No. But can they come here?" She waited. Knowing she was carrying a child made her realize just how much her need to see them and their reaction might hurt everyone involved.

He nodded slowly. "I will arrange it." He pulled her close, against his chest and she sighed. Her body hurt but right now she was safe and so was Galan.

And so too was their future child.

GALAN WAITED, tense and alert, watching as the vehicle carrying Jessa's parents drove through the gate. He had been aware of how they'd reacted so didn't wish to allow them aboard the *Princess Gospah*. Instead, he had arranged for them to meet at the facility where he had first met Jessa.

She was comfortable in that environment but close enough to their temporary home should he need any assistance. Seth had also made it clear that Jessa's mother could be difficult. He wasn't aware of all the reasons Galan had become so protective of her, but agreed with his planning.

The vehicle pulled up and he retreated inside, so they wouldn't see him before he was ready.

The woman alighted, smoothing her blonde curly hair down against the ravages of the wind. Her face was drawn and pale and she was tall, almost as tall as he was, Galan thought. Her curls sat tight around her head before disappearing into a tight knot at the back of her head and while she was thin, and no doubt perfect to many, she carried an air of brittleness around her like a cloak. He tensed sensing a formidable foe.

On the other hand, Jessa's father, Peter was round and shiny. With a bald spot on the top of his head and the wisps of gray hair looked natural. Far more so than the determinedly bright shades of blonde that Helen sported. He smiled but the woman at his side frowned in response.

They moved to the door and were met by several of his team, one stepped forward and Peter indicated the car and headed for the boot. Galan didn't stay to watch what they retrieved but hurried back to wait by Jessa's side.

"Are they here yet?" She shook a little with nerves and he grabbed her cool hand.

"Yes. Are you ready?" Jessa nodded and stood upright.

The door opened and her parents entered. Jessa moved a step closer and her father opened his arms. "Daddy. I missed you."

Galan relaxed a little.

"I missed you too, Jessa. I should never have... Well, it was wrong of me to say what I did."

Galan saw the fierce hug she gave her father.

Then she turned to her mother. "Mum?" She obviously meant to advance but the woman only returned a quick 'Hello,' and Jessa stilled.

Galan frowned seeing the hurt on Jessa's face, even though she covered it quickly. "Mum, I wanted you to meet..."

"The alien creature you've taken up with." Her voice was cold and forbidding and Peter looked at her, shocked.

"Helen... There's no need..."

Helen swung around and sneered at Peter. "Of course there is. Your daughter is abandoning her own race for this..." She waved a pointed finger at Galan and anger built. "...this creature."

"Mum! Galan is not an alien creature. You won't talk about him this way." Jessa retreated while Galan grabbed her hand, pulling her close to his side. Peter spun around and was about to say something when Helen spoke again.

"She's as bad as you. All pipe dreams and lovey dovey. No idea about realities of life and working. No, instead she got mixed up with that Jace and broke the law. It was bad enough taking her back after that. All my friends talked behind my back for years afterwards." She twisted back to Jessa with a spiteful look on her face. "But I knew the truth. You didn't even have the decency to leave home. No, instead you sullied the name you were born with and kept bringing it home with you."

Galan had heard enough. "Stop. Right. Now." He took a menacing step closer and Helen shrank back. She was like any other bully, looking to attack someone weaker and less able to defend herself. But she had taken on the wrong fight. No one spoke to Jessa like that.

"If you don't wish to be here, then leave. Jessa wanted to take the opportunity to bid you farewell, because she cared enough to say goodbye."

The woman watched his face, nervously licking her lips as if she realized she had gone too far.

"Either you say you appreciate her gesture and accept it for what it is or you leave."

He didn't need to say anymore. He knew his physical stature and position was enough to cow her. So he used it to advantage, staring hard at her until she agreed in silence and scooted for the door, moving with a jerky action as if trying to rein in her panic.

Peter stepped forward. "I need to apologize for my wife…"

Galan looked at the man, an air of sadness shrouded him.

"You should never apologize for your wife." Then he indicated the chairs where they could sit and talk.

PETER STAYED for several hours before rising in readiness to leave. He reached for Jessa and gave her a long hug. "Promise me you'll come back and see us."

Galan dipped his head in assent to Jessa's father, feeling pity for his obvious sadness at seeing Jessa leave. "She will. But it will be as my consort."

The man nodded slowly and shook his hand. He spun around and slowly left the room, glancing over his shoulder once and Galan detected the sheen of tears in his eyes. He and Jessa moved hand in hand to bid her father farewell, watching as the car sped down the drive.

"Thank you Galan. That was a great deal more difficult than I expected." Her voice was husky and he knew she was on the verge of tears once more.

He pulled her into his arms. "Your father is a good man. I wonder if he would accept an invitation to join us for a while on Hesparia. He might even bring your brother."

She laughed and clutched at him. "I hope so. I really do."

VEHICLES RUMBLED into the compound and women in giggling groups clambered down the steps in twos and threes. From the eli-pad Jessa watched as they made their way towards the ship.

Security teams darted here and there unloading the bus trailers of suitcases and boxes that were necessary to these new Hesparians. Some looked with shining eyes to the hull of the *Princess Gospah*. Others shook and shivered, pale and ill taking this final step. Jessa stepped up with a smile, feeling supremely confident in her role. She'd done this a number of times now and had her spiel down, almost pat.

"Welcome to the *Princess Gospah*. My name is Jessa and it's my honor, as the consort of Prince Galan to welcome you aboard." She moved among them, nodding to Joras to begin grouping them by the symbols on their official badges.

"Once we have you onboard, we will complete stowing away your items and get you settled. The initial transportation will only take around twelve hours and then you will be transferred to the ship that awaits you."

Galan stood quietly watching from the shade of the *Princess Gospah* as he usually did, during the welcoming proceedings. She smiled at one young woman who seemed so lost. It was a good thing all these women spoke English or she'd have a difficult time translating.

A car made its way up the drive and pulled in. Agent Foley climbed out and shook the hands of the driver then headed to the boot. *What on earth is he doing here now?*

The sound of so many voices, engines roaring and creaking wheels was incredible so she didn't hear Galan as he approached. "Who'd have thought? So he decided to accept my invitation."

She glanced over her shoulder, startled. "You asked him to come with us?" She searched his face looking for a clue as to why.

"I did. Actually I think it has more to do with the fact that his superiors thought he was totally compromised during his time with us. They wanted to dispense with his services." Galan's voice was filled with a mixture of glee and happiness.

She watched the giant of a man making his way towards them, pulling a small fold down trolley with a suitcase and several boxes carefully stacked on it.

"Prince Galan... Jessa..." He looked at them and smiled. "I'm ready."

Jessa bit her lip. *I've made no allocation for him aboard. Where on earth can I stash him?* Then she pulled herself up. *Where on the Princess Gospah?* She giggled just once at her thought then stopped and stepped close to peck Foley on the cheek. He blushed slightly and she grinned.

He was welcomed enthusiastically, well enthusiastic for the mild mannered Joras anyway, and Agent Foley accepted the praise with a small smile.

"Call me David," she heard Agent Foley exclaim to Joras and grinned, snuggling back into the quick embrace Galan offered.

"David. His name is David." Jessa smiled. Somehow it suited him. Suddenly realizing that the odd man joining their motley crew of migrants and runaways would fit in just fine.

She looked back to the ship, noting that the crowd had now dwindled. The eli-pad dropped back down and the women stepped up, some looking back and others she guessed were looking determinedly to the future. It rose quickly from sight. Jessa and Galan started walking back to the ship.

This time when the eli-pad descended she and Galan, David, Joras and the last of the women stepped aboard. Once they reached the corridor she headed to the meeting room and took her position at the front. She instructed the women on how to fasten their safety belts and settle in. A loud rumble filled the ship and the room turned silent. She smiled, knowing Galan had headed directly to the bridge to assume his position overseeing their ascent.

The walls glowed and Jessa depressed a button. "Ladies, I warmly welcome you to the adventure of a lifetime." A viewing window, previously hidden from their sight emerged and she heard gasps. On a screen, they watched as the ship left the ground, where the *Princess Gospah* had rested now showed only darkly scorched patches.

Some of the women started weeping softly and Jessa understood their distress. Yet others smiled and she shared their excitement. Gravitational forces pulled at them, shoving them back in their chairs. The view changed showing the earth falling away and gradually the viewer turned darker as did the scene outside the carefully reinforced window. Once freed from the atmosphere they were free to sit up and she unbuckled before getting up from her chair.

"Okay then, let's discuss billeting for all of you once we reach the other ship." She smiled and looked around. Soon they would be joined by the diplomats and those due to spend time on Hesparia. But these women would be her sisters and family.

Epilogue

Jessa lay on the bed, tired and a little pale but utterly delighted. In her arms lay twin babies. One girl and one boy. Both with the berry deep skin of native Hesparians, but with her green eyes and reddish blonde hair.

His heart was full of hope and joy.

Since her arrival, she'd worked tirelessly to settle the earth women on Hesparia, acting as an intermediary, counsellor and even, in some cases pseudo older sister. It hadn't been easy for anyone but she'd handled herself with grace at all times.

The citizens of Hesparia had been overjoyed when they announced the impending arrival of the children not long after landing and now the streets were decorated with bunting, as the entire planet celebrated the birth of the twins. The men had wept, but this time with happiness, to know that the genetic anomaly which had so nearly brought their planet to its knees would be arrested and overcome.

She looked up at him and his heart swelled. "So, I did okay, right?"

He grinned, unable to contain his reactions. He didn't even attempt to mitigate them. "You know you did well." She laughed at his words and winced as her body protested slightly. He smiled and sat down on the bed next to her and she handed him his son.

"Here take him. He's just fed and will go to sleep soon. Actually, take your daughter as well for a moment." He watched as she rose slowly then lifted the light wrap. She slipped it over her sleeping gown then cinched it lightly around her waist. "I'll take her now."

He watched as she beckoned him with her head. "What do you want?"

She laughed. "Well not that!" She laughed happily and moved to the window. "Open the shutters."

Galan looked confused. He cradled his newly born son but nevertheless flicked them open. She lifted their daughter. "This is your home Gelina. Say hello to Hesparia."

She could tell the instant he understood, raising his son, facing him to the town laid out below their window. "This is your home Peter. Say hello to Hesparia."

She looked back to see Galan smiling at him just as the door opened. His father, white haired but still tall and proud joined them. His pale eyes glowed with happiness as he touched each babe with a soft finger. Her daughter yawned and turned towards the touch.

"I bring news." Galan's father spoke quietly.

Jessa waited, knowing he meant the results of the genetic tests that had been run on the babies in their arms, her heart stuttering in her chest. "And?"

"The genetic abnormality does not exist in the babes. They are free of the taint."

Jessa grinned broadly. Her children would live a normal lifespan and her daughter... *their* daughter would be able to grow and marry. To bear children. As it was always meant to be. A glance at Galan showed his elation at this knowledge.

"My daughter, you have done very well indeed." A warm wave of pride filled Jessa as she reflected on the positive relationship she and Galan's father had formed. She knew he had noted her response.

"And you, my son, have a fine and good woman."

Jessa blushed slightly but remembered the actions of the people.

Every time they saw her they smiled and waved. No query was too big or too small. And every day she saw another aspect in the transformation of their dying culture. It had a new vibrancy as men smiled and laughed.

In the next few days her father would arrive from Earth with the new batch of diplomats who had come to take up their positions on Hesparia, the Hesparians having left some months before. Sadly her mother could not and would not set aside her bias but she banished that thought, focusing on the positive. Her father would meet his grandchildren. Children that would grow and flourish under the many suns of Hesparia.

As if there wasn't enough to celebrate, Seth and Danni would be making their commitments before their king tomorrow, the first of many that had been scheduled as men and women found their bonded partner.

But right now, all she could focus on was her own small family. And the knowledge that she was happy, knowing Hesparia's season of tears had passed.

IF YOU ENJOYED this book by Imogene Nix why not check out some more of her titles by scrolling through to the following pages?

Inheritance Of The Blood by
Imogene Nix

In the darkness evil waits...

As a young bride Kira was whisked away from everything and everyone she knew, including her new husband and became Christina, an operative of the Displaced Persons Unit.

As the danger grows she sees an opportunity to save her

husband Vasya and sister Serina. But nothing is the same. Serina is grown up—married and pregnant.

Vasya too is older and darkly forbidding. Trusting Christina doesn't come easily until a catastrophic event takes place. Now, knowing the truth everything he thought he knew is changed. But at a very high cost.

The four must work together to defeat the Demon, Zuor and the stakes are higher than they imagined and all could be lost.

The burning at the back of her neck warned she was being watched. A quick glance didn't clarify it. Instead, she turned around in time to see her mother's face, pale. "Mama?"

She took a step forward, but her grandfather snatched her wrist.

The grip was painful, and Kira stilled. "Let your parents talk."

She didn't know what the topic of conversation was, but it couldn't be good.

The dappled sunlight seemed cooler than before.

Her father crooked his forefinger at her grandfather while they stood there. For a moment she wished Vasya had come with them, but he had to work. Just the thought of her new husband warmed Kira.

She only had a few minutes to contemplate her newly defined status as a married woman, when her grandfather pulled at her hand. "Come with me." He tugged and, confused, Kira allowed herself to be towed away.

A glance at her parents' faces stole any feeling of well-being.

"Grandfather?"

"Shh, my love. You must go." His grip was implacable and his face stern, but he shivered.

"What are you doing? Where are you taking me, Grandfather?"

They moved rapidly through the village they'd visited to sell their wares just that morning, and for the first time since they'd arrived in the market place she felt fear. What was wrong? Was it something to do with Vasya?

"You are in danger. We must send you away." The words confused her further. Send her away? Danger?

"Where is Vasya?" She stumbled over a stone, but he kept tugging her onwards.

With a quick glance around, he hauled her into a dirty laneway between the buildings. Kira gasped, trying to drag air into her starving lungs. "There's no time. We must get you away."

A nondescript shopfront lay ahead, and he pushed on the door. It rattled and opened with a loud groan. "Andre? Andre, are you here?"

An older man shuffled into the room, bent nearly double from the weight of the load on his back. "Marat? What do you want?"

"My granddaughter. They are coming for her and us. Get her away. Take her now, while you can."

The man's face clouded over. "Are you sure?"

"Grandfather, where is Vasya?" Fright had the blood in her veins pounding.

"Hush, my precious. Andre will see you well." He turned. "Whatever it takes, Andre. Take her now." With surprising speed, her grandfather whirled and was gone.

The man, Andre, eyed her. "Come this way, child. There is no time to be lost."

Eleven years later

The tattoo of her heart and cry of terror woke her, as they usually did. Once again, as she had since that rapid flight from those who sought her, she found herself in a lonely bed. Hundreds of miles away from everything she'd dreamed of, in a house she'd built for them to share. As always, it left her wishing that Vasya had fled with her.

Instead, here she was, exiled without her husband. With a sob, she rolled over and let the tears fall.

Available from Love Books Publishing
books2read.com/IOTB

Direct Autographed Copy
http://bit.ly/2w6g4K6

The Celtic Cupid Trilogy

When Cupid—otherwise known as Diocail— is banished from his home on a remote Scottish Island, he's set a series of tasks by the great god Lugh, who also happens to be his father.

In **Blame The Wine**, he must bring two lovers together... BBW Cara and James, the man she's lusted over from afar who happens to be a super geek and head Veha Industries.

In **A Stranger's Embrace**, Diocail is driven to help an

emotionally fragile Jane and Davis, a famous author. The task is more complicated, with the existence of Carstairs her could-be ex-husband and teenage daughter, Frannie.

In **Revenge on Cupid**, Diocail must take the ultimate chance and find his own happily ever after with Simone. Sometimes the past gets in the way and HEA's don't come cheap though.

The dusty, dingy little diner was full, even with its current state of cleanliness—or lack thereof. People from the surrounding offices didn't care about anything except the incredible, well-prepared food at a reasonable cost. They flooded in, like waves to the shore. As one tide left, another swept in.

"Honestly, Simone. I'm going to try getting his attention one more time. If that doesn't work, I'm out of there. I mean, how long can I keep trying?" Cara picked at the caramel tart she hadn't been able to resist with the cheap metal fork and flicked the blob of fresh cream that sat on top to the side of the plate.

"You've said that tons of times before. Besides, what are you going to do to get his attention? Hmm? Walk naked through the typing pool?" Simone bobbed the straw in her smoothie as she eyed her friend with a frown. "It's been what? Eighteen months since you saw him, and you've mooned over him from a distance ever since you met him. You need to move on, Cara. That is, unless there's something you haven't shared?"

The query was arch. Cara shivered even as she shook her head. "No."

Simone quirked an eyebrow, obviously unconvinced with the answer. Cara let out a deep sigh of frustration. "There's a position...it's only temporary, for a PA reporting directly to him." She speared a forkful of tart, chewed quickly and swallowed, before continuing. "In his office, full-time for the period of the engagement. I saw the memo yesterday. I mean, I have the skills, right? I can type, answer phones, make coffee, file, greet people. What's more, I can probably do it better than all those size eights in the typing pool that Ms. Jackman seems to prefer." She nodded thoughtfully. "All I have to do is get past the ogre in Human Resources."

Simone stared at her, disbelief clear on her face. "Girl, I so remember that woman. If you think you can get past her, you're doing better than I ever did. That's why I left Veha Industries, remember? Maybe it's time to haul out your resumé and consider some other options. Look for something better." Simone shook her head and billows of her crimson hair swirled through the still air.

Cara understood Simone only had her best interests at heart. But this time she knew the outcome would be different. Hell, she could feel it in the air. The tingle of expectation.

"Cara, the HR ogre will hang you out for breakfast before she offers you anything like a position in that office. Remember her mantra? Good looks and good work make for a positive workplace!"

Simone didn't sugar-coat anything. It was another great reason for their long- term friendship. Honesty. But Cara didn't want to hear the truth in the statement. Even if it was exactly as her friend said.

Cara nodded quickly. "Yeah, I know, but if I don't try, then I won't know how close I can get to him, right? And the only way to catch his attention is to get past *her* and see him in person." Cara quaked a little at the information she needed to share. The favor she needed to ask. "Anyway, I tidied up my resumé and dropped the application into a memo envelope yesterday, so it's too late to back out now. I mean, fortune favors the brave. Doesn't it? If I don't snag an interview, I'm going to visit the career advisor across the street and register with them." She shrugged. "I'll look for temp work until something more long-term shows up. I can see what they have on offer and well...who knows? Maybe a job with the right boss is just waiting for me. But I'd rather this worked out, to be honest." Her voice trailed off into a whisper. "I really wish he would notice me."

Simone took a long slurp of her banana drink, and Cara noticed her questioning gaze even as she squirmed. Finally, Simone nodded. "It's your funeral. So anyway, you'd better show me this memo if you want me to be a referee for you. I'm guessing that's what you need, right? I'll have to know what I'm supposed to say about you before they ring."

Cara smiled. "Thanks, Simone. I knew I could count on you." She slipped a piece of paper out of her handbag and handed it over. "Sorry it's a bit creased. It was in the bottom of my bag, I stashed it so none of the others from the pool would see. You know how it is."

Available from Love Books Publishing
books2read.com/CelticCupid

Direct Autographed Copy
http://bit.ly/2vs7wtS

BioCybe by Imogene Nix

Can a cyber-enhanced warrior and a ship's captain find love together?

Levia Endrado never wanted to be a warrior, but at seventeen she was deemed suitable for battle. After intense training and multiple enhancements, which gave her superior strength and healing ability, she was sent off to defeat the enemy—a killing machine with a mission.

When the war was over, she had to find a new life. At twenty-seven she's a washed-up veteran without a future. Or she was, until she met Sandon Daria.

Serving as a pilot aboard Sandon's spaceship the *Golden Echo* makes Levia long for a different and gentler life. But old hurts and even older enemies aren't so easily forgotten. Particularly when they come back for her.

Sandon is determined to show Levia that she's more than just a BioCybe…she's the woman who completes him. Getting close is just the first step, keeping her alive is an even bigger challenge, but one he's willing to take because the prize is their combined future.

———————————

Levia scanned the long line of other hopefuls entering the chamber. The large building in the center of town was cold, and she dragged her wrap around her body, even as she craned her head, looking to the high ceiling. She'd never before had an occasion to enter the testing complex, yet she'd seen the lines of teenagers every time they passed the building.

Once she'd asked her parents why the teens were lined up and her mother's face had shuttered. Her stepfather had just shaken his head and growled. They'd stopped her questions with a carefully uttered, "You'll know soon enough, Levia." The pain in her mother's eyes had been enough to shush her questions. For endless months afterward, her parents had traveled different routes to the educational facility she attended and Levia lost interest in the puzzle of that building.

Now, as she looked around, remembering that long ago spring day, it was her opportunity to find out. But she felt a surge of concern at what lay ahead. She likely wasn't the only one, given that there were probably two to three hundred seventeen-year-olds gathered in the one place. Ahead of her, she caught sight of a couple of girls, their arms linked together and wide smiles on their faces.

Scanning the crowd, she became aware that, by far, a majority of those gathered displayed both fear and trepidation.

"All female subjects will enter through doors three, six, and seven. All male subjects will enter through gates four, eight, and ten." The speaker above her was loud, and she jumped before checking the numbers etched on the black metal sign over her head.

The massive doors beside her swung open, and now an uncertain silence reigned. Many of the youngsters hung back, clearly discomforted by whatever testing regime lay ahead. This was where they'd been told their futures would be determined.

"Oh gosh, I hope they only have an aptitude and psych eval. I don't think..." Levia turned to see the white face of the girl behind her. The girl had uttered what many must silently be thinking.

Levia dragged an unsteady breath in, her hand resting flat against the plane of her belly as she looked around. No one had entered yet. It was clear many were on the verge of taking the step, but still they hung back.

She straightened her shoulders. "I'm not afraid." It was always wiser to approach things head-on, she believed. When her biological father had died, she'd been one of the few to view his capsule before it was sent into the massive gray structure built to accommodate those who'd moved onto the next life realm.

Her legs shook as she wobbled toward the entrance. Beyond the doorway, she spied sealed cubicles and her heart stuttered. Why cubicles? Usually testing—med and psych—were in eval-units, hidden only by billowing white curtains. She glanced back, noting that others had taken the first step.

"Move along, subjects." Once again, the androgynous voice of the address system blared.

Of course, given it was her seventeenth anniversary of birth, she was technically considered an adult now.

She thought longingly of baby Rald and her half-sister, Elda, waiting at home for her to return, and the celebrations to be held that night. That made her smile. She would need to make them proud of her.

She entered a row and the tall Educational Specialist, the edu-specs as her peers laughingly called them, stopped her. "Present your credentials to the scanner."

She'd done this many times since the tiny implant had been slipped below the dermal layer of her skin at birth. The small unit in her wrist heated as her details were checked.

"Enter the first cubicle, Levia Endrado, and follow the instructions to complete your assessment."

Thus dismissed, Levia moved to the first unit, laid her palm against the scanner, and the door slid open soundlessly.

"Welcome, Levia Endrado. Take your place in the eval-unit." The soft contralto of the voice echoed after the door closed silently behind her.

"What are you evaluating?" Her voice was breathy, and she peered around.

"Your skills—physical and psychological. Your emotional and medical status. Your educational attainment levels."

It was an answer that shed little insight into the many things she was hungry to know. "Why do all seventeen year olds—"

"Take a seat, Levia. Then we may begin your testing."

If she'd expected an answer, she was sadly mistaken, she considered sourly. She dropped into the seat, the soft leather-like surface molding to her body.

"Levia Endrado, you are required to remove all non-specified apparel."

She jolted in the chair. "It's cold."

"The temperature will be amended. Remove the non-specified apparel."

Her misgivings grew as she dragged off the light wrap she'd brought with her, and then threw it to the floor at the side of the unit.

"We will begin, Levia Endrado. At any time, should you experience any malfunctions of the unit, simply depress the red button." It glowed and she grimaced.

Levia reclined against the chair and waited for the testing to begin.

The first examination was based on her understanding of the

political system, where she saw herself, and her knowledge of the rights and responsibilities accorded through citizenship of both her planet and the commonwealth.

The second test was mathematical and scientific proficiency. It felt like hours had passed by the time she'd finished, and she lay limp on the seat, exhausted.

"Levia Endrado, you may rise. The sanitary unit will emerge once you trigger the yellow button at the door. Should you require refreshment, press the blue button and a restorative will be made available."

"Can I leave?"

"Negative, Levia Endrado. Your needs will be catered for in this capsule."

"Why?" Her voice hitched and true fear rose for the first time. Why did they keep her in the alcove?

"All will be revealed at the end of the testing cycle."

Levia looked at the now empty screen before hurling a curse word. It was met with silence.

The urgent throb of her bladder reminded her that she needed to use the facilities, so, with

a sigh, she rose and clambered from the seat. After attending to the needs of her body, she walked around the unit, peering at the door, but it was obviously programmed remotely. She poked and prodded, but it made no difference. With a huff, she headed back to the chair.

The moment she'd settled in, the viewing screen shone bright. "Welcome back, Levia. The next sequence will evaluate your psychological reflexes, then that will be followed up with the general knowledge portion of the evaluation."

"When can I leave?" It seemed better to ask bluntly, she told herself.

"Once the examination is completed. After the next set of evaluations, you will be subjected to the physical aspect."

"Then I can go home?"

"Levia Endrado, you will now complete the psychological test. This will be undertaken by one of the center's personal evaluators."

She frowned. Personal evaluators? She bit her lip, and the sting reminded her that this wasn't something to joke about. In her seventeen years, she'd only heard of personal evaluators being brought in once before, and that was when one of the girls at her academy had been in a serious accident. Both legs were amputated and her body's ability to keep her alive had been gravely compromised. Her peers had been informed that the girl had requested the assessment before she could request her support systems be disconnected.

"Levia Endrado, are you ready to recommence processing?" The emotionless voice echoed once more and she gulped.

"Yes."

Available from Beachwalk Press
http://www.beachwalkpress.com

Direct Autographed Books
http://bit.ly/BioCybe

Also by Imogene Nix

Warriors of the Elector

- Star of Ishtar
- Starline
- Starfire
- Star of the Fleet
- Starburst
- The Star of Eternity

The Star of Ishtar & Starline - Print

Starfire & Star of the Fleet - Print

Starburst & The Star of Eternity - Print

Blood Secrets (Re-releasing 2020)

- The Blood Bride
- The Illuminated Witch
- The Sorcerer's Touch

The Search Duology

- Miss Elspeth's Desire
- Miss Isabelle's Craving (Not Yet Released)

Reunion Trilogy

- War's End
- The Assassin
- Executing Justice

The Reunion Trilogy in Paperback

Sex Love & Aliens

- Tangled Webs
- False Webs
- Covert Webs

21st Testing Protocol

- Cyborg: Redux
- Children Of A Greater Evil (Not Yet Released)
- When Evil Came To Stay (Not Yet Released)
- Finis: The War To End All Wars (Not Yet Released)

Celtic Cupid Trilogy

- Blame The Wine
- A Stranger's Embrace
- Revenge On Cupid

The Celtic Cupid Trilogy in Paperback (August 2019)

Zombieology

- The Reset (2018)
- I Dream of Zombies (Coming 2019)
- The Six Million Dollar Zombie (Not Yet Released)

Single Titles

The Chocolate Affair

A Sapphire for Karina

BioCybe

Hesparia's Tears

Tomorrow's Promise

A Bar In Paris

Inheritance Of The Blood

The Plan

Loving Memories

Hero of Heartbreak Hill

Raspberry Dreams (Not Yet Released)

Non Fiction

Self Publishing: Absolute Beginners Guide (With Suzi Love)

Written as Ciara Cave

25 Curated Ways To Get Rid Of Telemarketers

Book Signings for Absolute Beginners

About the Author

Imogene is published in a range of romance genres including Paranormal, Science Fiction and Contemporary. She is mainly published in the UK and USA.

In 2010, Imogene Nix (the pen name not Imogene herself) was born. Imogene sat down and worked tirelessly for 3 months culminating in the book Starline, which became the first in a trilogy titled, "Warriors of the Elector." Since then she's had over 30 titles published and is now focusing on hybridising herself - with a mixture of traditionally published and self-published works.

In fact, she's taking control of many of her back catalogue books, which are slowly re-releasing as self-published titles.

Imogene is a member of a range of professional organisations world wide, and believes in the mantra of mentoring and paying it forward and is actively involved in mentorship (through NaNoWrimo and her vlog: In The Chair With Imogene Nix) and tutoring of new and upcoming authors.

In her spare time she loves to drink coffee, wine & eat chocolate and is parenting her spoiled dog and a ferocious cat along with her husband and 2 human daughters and looks forward to weekends away with her husband in their caravan "The Seven Year Hitch!" Do look forward to her caravan romance at some point!

To Contact Imogene

www.imogenenix.net
imogene@imogenenix.net

facebook.com/ImogeneNix

twitter.com/ImogeneNix

instagram.com/ImogeneNix

www.ingramcontent.com/pod-product-compliance
Lightning Source LLC
Chambersburg PA
CBHW031952130726
47905CB00003BA/762